THE
HUSBAND

BOOKS BY DANIEL HURST

The Holiday Home
The Couple's Revenge
The Family Trip

THE PERFECT NURSE SERIES
The Perfect Nurse
The Nurse's Lie
The Nurse's Mistake

THE DOCTOR'S WIFE SERIES
The Doctor's Wife
The Doctor's Widow
The Doctor's Mistress
The Doctor's Child

THE
HUSBAND

DANIEL HURST

Bookouture

Published by Bookouture in 2025

An imprint of Storyfire Ltd.
Carmelite House
50 Victoria Embankment
London EC4Y 0DZ

www.bookouture.com

The authorised representative in the EEA is Hachette Ireland
8 Castlecourt Centre
Dublin 15 D15 XTP3
Ireland
(email: info@hbgi.ie)

ISBN: 978-1-83618-367-9
eBook ISBN: 978-1-83618-366-2

PROLOGUE

Nobody's husband is perfect.

Every wife likes to think their man is the exception, right up until the moment they realise the person they stood beside at the altar has his flaws too. For me, that realisation came recently and, when it did, I was as surprised as every other poor woman who has been in that position before me.

No, that's not right. I wasn't only surprised. It was way more than that. That's because I didn't only find out that my husband had a few weaknesses or bad habits. Those could be forgiven and worked on. What I discovered about my husband went way beyond surprise. I was shocked, stunned, shaken to the core.

And most of all, afraid.

Very, very afraid.

That's because my husband's imperfection was something so big that not even a simple request for a divorce could have saved me from the horror of it. Nor would a separation have saved our two darling children either, our son and daughter, the kids that are the fruits of our once-happy union. But like any tree from which fruit can grow, the roots can wither and die, and that's what has happened to my relationship with my husband.

But it's not my fault.

It's all on him.

The man I share my bed with.

The man I had two children with.

The man I call my husband.

And the man who currently has my family trapped.

We're trapped because I fear he will do anything to keep his secret safe. But I will do anything to keep my children safe, so something has to give. Only one of us can get what we want. One of us will win and one of us will lose.

I guess that's no different to the end of most marriages.

Except mine is different.

Mine will end in murder.

ONE

JENNY

All the family are around the table. Is there any better sight for a mother than that?

As I look around over the sea of warm plates, hot dishes full of food and glasses full of soft drinks or something alcoholic, I smile as it can only mean one thing: it's dinnertime and my husband and two children are here with me – safe and happy.

But while my heart is at peace, the conversation is more turbulent.

'Urgh, move up, you're on my side of the table,' my daughter, Bonnie, complains to her brother, William. He's always been known to spread out and take up a lot of space, from when he was a toddler sharing a bed with me in the middle of the night to now; he is a rapidly growing teenager getting taller by the day.

He responds in typical sibling fashion, meaning rather than do what his sister wants, he chooses to impose on her personal space even more before eventually elbowing her in the ribs.

'Ouch,' Bonnie moans as she wriggles away from him, which is music to her brother's ears because it means he has won this particular battle and when it comes to these two, there's always a battle to be fought and won. That doesn't mean they don't love each other. As two teenagers living under the same roof, they are bound to butt heads regularly as they fight for not just their place at this kitchen table but where they might fit into life itself as they get older.

Bonnie is seventeen, so she'll have to figure that out a little sooner than William, who is a couple of years younger, but whatever they go on to do as they grow up, I will make sure they know that they will always have a place here. Right now, it's their places around this table that are posing a problem, and I have no idea why William has sat so close to his sister, unless it really is simply to wind her up.

'Just move up!' Bonnie cries again, and just before her brother goes to teasingly elbow her one more time, I try to nip this in the bud.

'Guys, please! Stop messing around!'

It's never fun when I have to raise my voice to restore some order, but it's also never fun to listen to two people squabbling when you're tired, and I am certainly tired after a day of running errands for my family. I'm not the only one either. My husband, Lachlan, has been at work all day and as it's not even Wednesday yet, he still has a while to go until the weekend. Though I don't have a day job like him, I'm tired myself, as running this household is a full-time occupation. But whereas I tend to thrive in the chaos that is our family, Lachlan needs some respite from it every now and again.

'The chicken's perfect. Really tender,' my man says from the other end of the table, and I smile following his compliment on my cooking. Before I can thank him or pass comment on my cooking method that made the chicken turn out so well, William speaks up again.

'Yeah, it's good, Mum. Not dry like when Dad cooks it.'

'That's one thing we can agree on,' Bonnie replies, and as I laugh, Lachlan feigns hurt.

'Hey! I'm not that bad of a chef, am I? You all loved the meatballs I made the other week!'

'Yeah, but it's still better when Mum cooks,' Bonnie says before adding a comment that instantly makes my heart sting. 'I'll miss this when I'm at uni.'

There it is. The dreaded word that has been hanging over my life recently, ever since my daughter decided that she was planning to go on to higher education. It's not that I'm unhappy at her decision to go to university. I'm certainly not disappointed in her chosen subject, which is Health & Social Care, because that will potentially lead her on to a fantastic career that she will enjoy and thrive in. She's always been a caring soul, when she's not teasing her brother, so I was not shocked when she told me she wished to pursue a qualification that would allow her to work with those who need care the most. What I am disappointed about is the fact that her chosen university, and the one she will be starting at if she gets the exam results she is predicted to get, is over one hundred miles away from here. Our family home is in Preston, a very normal, working-class city in the north, but Bonnie plans to go south, to Nottingham, a place she perceives to be more exciting than home and maybe it is for a young woman like her. That means she'll be living there, on campus, for the next three years, rather than here, in this house, where she has been for the past seventeen.

I know it's important that she flies the nest and gains some independence. But it's also important that I don't spend every day before then wallowing in the loss I am about to feel when she moves out and there is an empty seat at this table every night. As for the anxiety I feel about her being away and not always knowing what she might be doing and if she's okay, that's something I'll have to deal with on my own. It's not her fault I'm nervous about her venturing out into the world – she's simply doing what all children do when they grow up. And like all mothers before and after me, I'm doing what I should be doing about that – namely, *worrying about it*.

Maybe it really is a normal part of life. Or maybe I'm worried that my family has been absolutely perfect for all this time and surely our luck can't last. Is that a thing? Could our luck run out? Could our perfect family unit be destroyed in some awful, unforeseen way? Or am I really letting my overactive imagination run away with itself?

'Hello? Earth calling Mum? Are you there?'

I snap out of my trance to see my son is trying to get my attention.

'Sorry, what was that?' I ask as he rolls his eyes at me.

'Have we got any more potatoes?'

I smile and get up from my seat before taking the empty bowl that was brimming with potatoes only fifteen minutes previously and going in search of some more. I always make extra because, at fifteen, William is a growing boy and thanks to all the football he plays, he is constantly hungry. But it's not only him who eats like a horse around here. My husband is prone to overfilling his plate too, so between them, the males in this family ensure the grocery shopping bill only ever goes up, not down. Bonnie is more like me, she eats little and often, preferring to nibble on the go rather than eat a huge meal in one sitting, which is why the pair of us have already finished eating for now. Although I'm sure we will soon be opening a box of chocolates while we're watching TV together later.

It's another reminder of why I'm going to miss her so much. We're similar, while William takes after his father more. But life has a way of balancing things out, which is why I'm then reminded of something I won't miss.

'Hey! Get off, that's mine!' Bonnie cries, and I turn around to see her trying to get her drink back from William, who seems to have picked up her glass and is finishing it for her.

'Snooze, you lose.' William laughs before thirstily gulping

down his sister's drink. He must have already finished his own and rather than get himself another, he's chosen the easy option.

'You're so annoying!' Bonnie tells him loudly before trying to hit his arm, but he expertly dodges the punch, years of muscle memory coming into practice.

'Guys, please! Settle down!'

Lachlan's voice is louder than everyone else's, and usually does the trick, and this time is no different. William stops messing around, and Bonnie stops trying to hit him and, for a brief period, order has been restored.

'More potatoes,' I say as I deliver the dish to the table, and William eagerly shovels several onto his plate before Lachlan picks up the spoon and does the same. As the two males discuss the upcoming football game that is on TV tonight, and while Bonnie checks the messages on her mobile phone that seems to be surgically attached to her hand, I take a sip of my wine and smile. I could try and steer the conversation onto a topic for all of us rather than football, which bores me, or I could remind Bonnie that she shouldn't be using her phone at the table, which will annoy her. But I don't do those things. Instead, I sit and enjoy this life that Lachlan and I have created for ourselves.

When I first met my husband on a hot and sweaty nightclub dancefloor, we were two people in our early twenties who didn't even know what we wanted in life, let alone how to look after the two children we would eventually have. When it was only the two of us, our days consisted of so much romance – dates, holidays, lazy Sundays and long evenings that seemed to drift on forever as we listened to music, drank too much alcohol and kissed passionately. Things changed a lot when I found out I was expecting Bonnie, and they've never gone back to the way they were all these years later, but I don't expect them to, nor should they. We are both forty now, which means we have changed a lot since our youth. We've grown up, we had no choice but to, but that doesn't mean we aren't still happy.

I love being Lachlan's wife as much as I love being the mother of his children and, one day, when it's just us two in this house again, I'll love all the adventures we can have together while the kids embark on their own. But for now, I consider life to be perfect and if I could freeze life and stay in this time forever, I actually think I would do it.

All four of us here, at this table. Me rushing around making sure everyone has enough food. William doing a very good job of eating all that food. Bonnie counting down her days to independence but still very much a mum's girl when the mood strikes her. And at the head of the table is my husband, working hard for us, keeping us all in check, and being the best father and provider he can be.

I don't even need to say that he's the best husband, as that's a given.

I struck gold when I found him, the handsome Scotsman on an English dancefloor.

I don't want either of us to age because that inevitably means one of us has to depart this marriage at some point many years from now, and I always want the two of us to be together. So yes, I would freeze time if I could.

The future can only spoil things, right?

Wrong.

The secrets of the past have the power to ruin everything...

TWO

LACHLAN

'Just don't let your mother find out.'

I make sure my son has understood my instructions before I open a cold bottle of beer for him and hand it over. At fifteen, William shouldn't be drinking yet, at least in the eyes of the law, but I've never let the law get in the way of a good time and I don't intend to start now. However, while I might not fear the repercussions of my son drinking this beer from the police, I do fear them from my wife, which is why I'd prefer for her not to find out that it's not only me who will be enjoying an alcoholic drink during the football game this evening.

I follow my son into the den, the cosy room at the back of our house where us males tend to go while the females of the house have commandeered the larger living area, and I think about how so much in my life has been about never letting my wife find out exactly what I'm up to.

Sure, this is only one beer, so if Jenny finds out about it then it won't be the end of the world. But if she finds out about the other things, the things I've kept hidden for years? It's safe to say that if that happened, things could never be the same again. There would be no more nights in this cosy den for me, watching football with my teenage son and savouring a satisfactory beer after a hard day's work. Instead, I'd be sitting in a barren prison cell with no refreshments, no entertainment, and most of all, no family.

'It's starting,' William says as he energetically leaps onto one end of the sofa to watch the game, while I wearily slump down on the other end. Oh, to be young and full of energy again. I remember fifteen. It was a tricky age, but it was certainly more fun than forty. In fact, I'd go so far as to say that the highlight of my life occurred when I was around my son's age, which is sad because that's twenty-five years ago now. The bigger problem is that it's a highlight only I know about. If I told anyone about what I'd done back then, it would only serve to make me a highlight on the next news bulletin.

'Why's he playing? He's ancient,' William says, pointing at the player on screen who he clearly thinks is past his best.

'Ancient? He's only thirty-six,' I reply, shuddering at the thought that my son considers a man who is four years younger than me to be old and decrepit. Then again, in sports terms, being in your mid-thirties does usually mean a player is on the wane so I understand his point. Still, it's not nice for anybody to be accused of being past their peak, though my son won't understand that yet.

As I sip my beer and watch the early stages of the game unfold, I begrudgingly ponder the concept that my peak was many, many years ago and all I have to look forward to now is a sense of growing regret as I get older. But it's not regret about what I've done in the past. It's more the regret that I will get fewer opportunities to repeat the things I consider to be in my highlight reel, and perhaps, I'm already physically incapable of doing so.

As the game unfolds, it's unpredictable, which is why so many people, including my son and I, love watching it as a spectacle. Although the more drama there is on the screen, the more frustrated I feel about how my life these days differs so much. There's no drama for me, no twists and turns, no thrills or anxiety. Just the same mundane routine, repeated until retirement. I guess I've done what most other guys my age have done. Got a job, got married, had kids, sat on the sofa and slowly put on weight before eventually succumbing to something like we all have to. I might not be overweight yet, despite how much cooking my wife does, but that's only because I run regularly and try to play football whenever the niggling injuries don't hold me back. But regular exercise is hardly a ticket to non-stop fun and entertainment, so while I might be delaying the ageing process slightly, what good is it if I'm bored and feel like the best is behind me?

I wasn't always like this. There was a time once when my life was as drama-filled as a fast-paced game of football. Alas, the real world has a way of keeping a person's hopes and dreams in check, which is why I have rarely been able to repeat what I did so well in the past.

In my case, the reason for me mostly abstaining from the fun I once had is due to the consequences should I ever get caught. I'm not talking about drinking too much and having to deal with worsening hangovers that affect my ability to work, or gambling with money that me and my family cannot afford to lose. Those are vices that ordinary people might have, but I'm not ordinary. I'm not even talking about having an affair, chasing the thrill of a woman other than my wife, knowing that the main consequence of getting caught is a legal separation and only seeing my kids every other weekend from then on. That's another vice that some men live for, but it is not what gets me going.

No, I'm very, very different. While other men do things that might put them in the majority, I'm in the minority. My pleasure in life is almost unspeakable. It certainly is if I want to keep my freedom. But as well as staying hidden from the police, my secret needs to stay hidden from my family if I ever want to see the adults that my children grow into. There's no doubt they'd cut me off if they knew the truth about their dad. Then there's Jenny, my loving wife, the woman who seems to worship the ground I walk on for no other reason than for the fact that I'm still with her. If she ever knew what I'd done, and if she ever knew what I'd love to do again in the future, she would leave me. But only after she had been sick, cried her eyes out and screamed at the heavens about how it was possible for a man like me to be so close to her and our children for so many years.

'What a goal!' William cries as he leaps up off the sofa and celebrates, and I have to pretend like I didn't miss it while thinking about the difficult problem in my life.

'Brilliant,' I say before swigging my beer again, only to realise that I've already finished it.

I may get another one, but no more than two tonight. I can keep my drinking in moderation, like I can keep my other vices in boring moderation too.

Two beers.

Two bodies.

As William retakes his seat on the sofa, I feel like throwing this empty bottle at the wall in frustration. I don't. I'm better than that. I excel in keeping calm. At not drawing attention to myself. At going under the radar. I'm just an average guy.

No one would ever suspect me of doing anything wrong and that's by design.

That's how I have been able to do this for so long.

That's how I have been able to get away with murder.

THREE

JENNY

'Not another murder mystery,' I groan when I see what my daughter has selected for us to watch this evening. While it might be better than the football that is currently showing on the television in the den, I'd still prefer to watch something a little more light-hearted as I wind down before bedtime. But true to her tastes, or the constantly changing tastes of an ever-evolving teenager, Bonnie has decided that of all the things we could watch tonight, it's a documentary about the murder of a woman in Scotland that has her attention.

'It's supposed to be really good,' Bonnie says as she presses Play on the remote control without any further debate.

'How can it be really good? It's about somebody dying,' I remind her, though I know she didn't mean anything by it. Rather, she's going off what the reviews say, or perhaps, what all her friends say if they are watching this too.

'You enjoyed the last documentary we watched,' Bonnie says then as the TV screen goes momentarily dark and we wait for this new documentary to begin.

'Enjoyed might be a strong word considering it was about a

man in America who killed three of his wives and ended up being executed,' I say with a jovial shake of the head. 'Seriously, I'm starting to worry about you and the things you watch.'

'True crime docs are the best,' Bonnie says before shushing me because the next one is about to start.

As it does, I briefly reflect on the many things I have watched with my daughter during her life. From animated cartoons when she was a tiny toddler, to silly shows when she was a small schoolgirl, as well as the mandatory dozens and dozens of Disney movies. Some mothers might get bored of watching the same things on repeat, and hearing the same songs over and over again on screen, but I never did. That's because one of the absolute joys of parenting for me has been to snuggle up on the sofa beside my children and watch something with them that gives them joy. But now, at seventeen, my daughter's tastes have changed quite dramatically and that means her favourite things to watch have changed too. Gone are the fluffy characters and nonsensical songs and in their place are shows in which a narrator discusses various grim facts about a real-life murder investigation.

I guess it's normal for youngsters to eventually develop a morbid curiosity or fascination with death, especially after so many years of watching light and breezy shows about talking animals and toys that can come to life. I know I shouldn't be too concerned that my daughter is intrigued by true crime to the point where her favourite way to end the day is by viewing documentaries about killers and their victims. I know all her friends like it too, as well as plenty of adults, if the sheer volume of these shows available to watch these days is anything to go by. They are not what I would choose to watch, though. Give me a melodramatic soap opera featuring the same safe characters getting up to risk-free mishaps every week, or a cheesy rom-com where everybody lives happily ever after. Those are the kinds of things I like to watch, the fictitious shows where nobody dies and nothing is real. The way I see it, there's enough doom and gloom in the world without inviting it into your own home. But if I want to spend as much time with my daughter as possible before she goes to university, and I really, really do, I guess this is how I am going to be spending most of my evenings until she leaves.

As the documentary begins, I see sweeping views of the majestic Scottish countryside, though the dark clouds and the sinister music that plays over the footage are foreboding and, sure enough, it seems this spectacular scenery hides a dark secret.

'At fifteen years old, Paisley Hamilton had her whole life ahead of her,' the male narrator tells the viewer. 'She dreamt of leaving the small Scottish village where she grew up and experiencing life in a big city. She'd mentioned Edinburgh. London. Even as far afield as Sydney. She had big dreams and everything to live for. That was until her body was discovered one rainy September morning in 2000, resulting in a murder investigation that not only shocked local residents at the time but left both them and the police dumbfounded as to why anyone would hurt such an innocent member of the community. Just as shocking as the act itself, the crime remains unsolved to this day, meaning Paisley's killer has never been brought to justice. Now, as the twenty-fifth anniversary of her murder approaches, we try to piece together what might have happened that night in one of the sleepiest villages in Scotland.'

My daughter opens a bag of popcorn and shoves a handful of salty snacks into her mouth, as casually as if she was watching the latest blockbuster movie in the cinema. She's grazing like always, though when she offers me the bag, I decline, even though I'm partial to a bit of popcorn too. It's not just because I feel it is a little inappropriate to snack on food while watching a documentary about a young girl being murdered, though it is jarring as she died at the same age as my son is now. But the main reason I'm not tucking into the snacks is that it seems the setting for this story is a place I am familiar with and it has shocked me. A second later, Bonnie realises it too.

'Carnfield? Isn't that where Dad's from?' Bonnie asks with a mouthful of popcorn. Rather than remind her that it's not a polite way to behave, I am focused on the TV. My daughter is right. The village where this murder apparently took place is indeed the village where my husband grew up.

'Yeah,' I say as I keep watching, and now we're being shown a few shots of the village itself in the modern day, well after the crime occurred, though I only know that as the narrator is telling us this, not because I've been there and seen it for myself.

'He must know about this then?' Bonnie suggests. 'He would have been a kid at the time. Wait, he'd have been fifteen. Same age as her. Oh my god, do you think he knew her?'

'I don't know,' I reply before considering going to get Lachlan and asking him. Although he'll be engrossed in the football game with William, so I don't want to interrupt them and spoil their boys' night. I'll ask him later.

'I have to tell my friends,' Bonnie says as she drops the popcorn and picks up her phone; her fingers start typing furiously on the screen. 'They've all been talking about this documentary, so they'll go mad when I tell them that my dad knew the victim.'

'He might not have known her,' I suggest, but in this rare instance, my daughter probably speaks more sense than me and she backs it up with her next point.

'It's a tiny village. If they were the same age then they would have been in the same class at school,' she says. I can't argue with that.

She's right. Lachlan must have known Paisley, this poor girl who, unlike my husband, never had the chance to grow up and spread her wings beyond the place of her birth. He's never mentioned her, though, not that such a thing is odd, as he's never been one to talk much about his childhood or the village where he grew up. Whenever I asked, which I did a lot when we first met and when I was doing my best to get to know him, he simply said the small village and everybody in it was boring, and he was glad to have left and moved to England. He's never gone back. His parents passed away before we met and he has no siblings, and so me and the kids have never been there either. I have suggested we go before, though, on the few occasions we've taken a short family vacation in Scotland, but he's always said there's no point going back to the place where he grew up because there's nothing to see, and no one to visit.

Basically, he's always made his village sound like the most uninteresting place on Earth. But if that's the case, why is it the setting for this documentary about an unsolved murder? I'll have to ask him when the football match is finished. But for now, I'll watch this documentary and learn more about this case because I know absolutely nothing about it. It must have been reported in the news, but maybe it only received coverage in Scotland. Would English media consider it newsworthy for those this side of the border? Possibly not. We have plenty of our own murders and mysteries on our side to report on.

Or maybe it *was* widely reported here, but I'd have been a teenager myself at the time and like most teens, I wasn't occupied with keeping up with current affairs. I couldn't have cared less what was going on in the world at that age. My life revolved around celebrity crushes, surviving schoolwork and doing my best to fit in among my peers. Only now I'm much older do I keep abreast of goings on in the news, mostly so I'm up to date and able to join in conversations with friends whenever the topic goes on to politics, A-list actor scandals or general local news. But also, I guess, I have two children, and I need to know precisely how dangerous the world is at any given moment.

Despite my initial reluctance to watch this, I'm quickly finding myself drawn in to learn more, so I guess my daughter was right.

True crime documentaries can be fascinating, after all.

FOUR

LACHLAN

Considering how unhappy I've been while contemplating my mundane, repetitive life, I am happy to see my team win. That means my boy William is happy too and, as I turn the TV off, he cheekily suggests we have one more beer to celebrate.

'No chance. You've got school in the morning,' I remind him as we get up from the sofa. 'And remember, don't tell your mother about the beer you've had or that's it until you're eighteen.'

'Okay,' William begrudgingly mumbles as we leave the den and pass through the kitchen.

While my son carries on through the house, I stop to deposit the empty beer bottles in the recycling bin. I don't expect my wife to go snooping in here, but if she does happen to see the bottles and asks me about them, I'll say that I consumed them all. She might not be overjoyed to learn that I had multiple beers on a weeknight at home, because that could be the start of a bad habit of drinking too much, especially when I tend to overindulge at the weekends, anyway. But it's preferable to her knowing I gave our son a sneaky beer, so it will remain our little secret.

Secrets.

Some people hate having them.

But for me, they make life interesting.

With the evidence disposed of, I follow William out of the kitchen and find him in the living area where Jenny and Bonnie are curled up on the sofa, an empty bag of popcorn lying between them.

'How are my girls?' I ask casually, checking in with them before I head upstairs to bed, which is where we should all be going soon considering the early start we have in the morning.

'Dad! Why have you never told us about Paisley?' Bonnie asks, and for a brief second, I swear my heart stops beating.

Why the hell has my daughter just said that name?

'Excuse me?' I reply as casually as I can muster.

'The girl who was murdered in Carnfield. Why didn't you tell us? Did you know her? She was the same age as you. You must have met her? What happened?'

Bonnie's questions are as unrelenting as her excitement, and I have to be careful not to get carried away like she clearly has.

Keep calm, I remind myself. That strategy has worked for me so far and it will hopefully work for me now, during this. *Whatever this is.*

'Sorry, what are you talking about?' I ask.

'Her!' Bonnie says, pointing to the screen and, when I look, I see a face that has come to me in my dreams on many a night over the last twenty-five years.

'Did you know her?'

That question came from my wife but I delay answering this too.

'What is this?' I ask, deflecting the questions with one of my own and trying to fathom how the past could have infiltrated my home so easily when I've done such an excellent job of keeping it out so far.

'It's a true crime documentary about the murder of Paisley

Hamilton and it happened where you grew up,' Bonnie tells me. 'So, did you know her or what?'

I turn away from the TV and to my wife and daughter who are looking to me for an answer while William picks up the popcorn bag only to be disappointed.

'Erm, no, I didn't know her,' I say before grabbing the remote control and turning the TV off.

'Hey! I was watching that!' Bonnie cries, reaching for the remote, but I keep it away from her, something I've done many a time as a parent.

'It's time for bed,' I say as I wait for everyone to head for the door. 'You've got college in the morning, your brother's got school and I've got work. So stop messing around and go upstairs.'

'I'm seventeen! I don't have to go to bed early anymore,' Bonnie tries. I can sense that William is about to take his sister's side for once and try and argue back with her, so I nip it in the bud quickly.

'I'm not asking you; I'm telling you. Now go,' I insist, the volume of my voice rising every time I have to speak.

'Urgh, this is so unfair. I can't wait to go to uni. I can stay up as late as I want to there and there's nothing you can do about it!' Bonnie cries as if she has won by saying such a thing.

But, fed up with this kind of behaviour at such a time of day, I snap back, tiredness, as well as my competitive side in this argument, getting the better of me.

'I don't care what you do when you're there, but while you're living under my roof, you follow my rules,' I tell her firmly. 'Now go!'

I point to the door and, with a lot of huffing and puffing, Bonnie gives up and goes, closely followed by her brother. I feel a slight pang of guilt because of course I care about what my daughter will be doing while she's at university, but in that split-second, I saw a way to maybe not win the argument, but at least not lose it, so I said what I said. Now it's over and that just leaves Jenny on the sofa. It doesn't take me long to notice that she is frowning at me.

'What's wrong? She was only asking you if you knew who Paisley was. There's no need for you to raise your voice at her. And we haven't told them to go to bed like that in a long time. They're older now, not little kids. We have to treat them differently.'

'I'm going to bed,' I reply, not wanting to get into a parenting debate at this time of night, so I walk away, although I know it'll only be a short reprieve because Jenny will inevitably follow me up to the bedroom.

By the time she comes up the stairs, I'm in bed and hoping to turn the lights off and get some sleep without any more discussion, but there's little chance of that.

'What's wrong?' Jenny asks me, standing by the bed.

'Nothing. I'm just tired.'

'No, it's something else. I know you.'

If only she knew how little that was true.

'I'm fine,' I say.

'No, you're not. Tell me.'

'Please, can we just go to sleep? I'm exhausted,' I try.

'Not until you tell me what is going on. You don't usually react like that, not over television, anyway. I don't want you to speak to Bonnie like that, not when she's so close to moving out, because if you do, she'll never want to come back and visit.'

'Oh, she'll be back, all right, either for money or food, but she'll come back.'

'What is going on?' Jenny asks, appearing concerned. 'You never talk like this. Tell me.'

I let out a deep sigh while racking my brains for something I can say that will get my wife to drop this. But Jenny has always been a stubborn soul, so I don't like my chances of achieving that very much.

'Is it the documentary? The one about Paisley?' she asks then, annoyingly guessing right.

'No, of course not.'

'It is, isn't it? You seemed to be annoyed that we were watching it. Why is that? Is it because you knew her?'

'I told you downstairs that I didn't know her.'

Jenny thinks on that and pauses before speaking again.

'It's a tiny village, Lachlan, and you were the same age as her when she died so you would have gone to school together. You must have known her.'

I realise that feigning ignorance about Paisley is not going to work for me, so I need to shift gears quickly.

'Okay, fine. I knew her,' I admit.

'Why did you say you didn't?'

'Because it's a long time ago and it's a horrible thing that happened to her, so I'd rather not dredge it all up,' I say then, which instantly causes my wife to soften.

She takes a seat on the edge of the bed beside me and now looks less annoyed.

'Are you okay?' she asks gently.

'Yes, I'm fine. You know I don't like talking about that place. I wasn't happy there, which is why I left, and my life has been so much better since. End of story.'

'I understand that, but Bonnie was only curious, and she has a right to be, as she knows you grew up there.'

'She shouldn't be watching things like that, and you shouldn't be encouraging her.'

'All her friends are watching it,' Jenny replies, as if that makes it okay.

'I don't care what her friends are doing. I care about our daughter and I'd rather she wasn't watching documentaries about dead people.'

'She's practically an adult now, so she can watch what she likes. And she's going to when she's not here, so I thought it's better to show an interest in what she likes rather than not spend time with her.'

'Okay, fine. Whatever. Can we please go to sleep now? You know I have to be up early.'

Jenny can't argue with that because while she doesn't have to go to work, I do, so she turns off the light and gets into the bed next to me. I feel her put an arm over me, but don't bother turning around and reciprocating, preferring to lie facing away from her and not have any more interactions this evening. Eventually, she removes her arm, wishes me goodnight and rolls over so our backs are touching. A while after that, I hear her soft snores. She's asleep, but I am wide awake. That's because I have a lot to think about.

I can't believe they've made a damn documentary about Paisley. Of all the murders in all the world, why this one? Then again, this year is the twenty-five-year anniversary of her murder, so I guess that has something to do with it. The police, as well as Paisley's parents, are still desperate for answers. But I have made sure they will never get them. I try to reassure myself that whatever the documentary is saying, it will only be going over things that are already public knowledge. It won't have any new insight or evidence to bring to light. If it did, I expect I would have received a visit from the police by now. But they haven't been to my door, and I'd like to keep it that way.

I've got away with killing Paisley for this long.

Surely my luck isn't about to run out anytime soon.

Right?

FIVE

JENNY

The house is quiet, which is not the way I like it. I like my house to be filled with noise and people, but it is a weekday, so the rest of my family members are occupied elsewhere. Lachlan left early this morning with Bonnie and William, dropping them at college and school before carrying on to work, as is the normal routine. That left me to get started on all the jobs I had to get done, but it's been a productive morning so far and I'm well ahead of schedule. I should be really because, after so many years, I have it down to a fine art. Some people might get overwhelmed at the sight of an untidy home, a full washing basket, a long shopping list and countless other tasks that all go into ensuring the smooth running of a busy household. But not me. I switch into 'Super Mum' mode and get everything done quickly, not just because I'm well versed in it now, but because the sooner I'm done, the sooner I can sit down with a cup of tea before the noisy herds return.

With the fridge full from this morning's shop trip, the clean washing drying out on the line in the back garden, and every room tidied up and looking respectable again, I'd say it's time for that much-sought-after liquid refreshment.

As the kettle boils, I stare out of the kitchen window and while the garden is empty now, barring the washing fluttering in the breeze, I can picture my kids out there when they were younger, running around on the grass. William was usually kicking a ball, which Lachlan loved because he saw that as easy playtime, while Bonnie would be pottering around by the flowerbeds. She was always a delicate girl, and I would love it when she would carefully pick a flower for me and bring it in, proudly delivering it and telling me to put it in water before running back outside to get one more. I didn't have the heart to tell her that she'd probably just killed the flower she had picked by ripping it from its root, because she thought she was doing something kind, and she was.

Now look at her. Seventeen and soon to leave.

I feel bad, not only because my kids are growing up and leaving soon, but also because of the argument last night. Lachlan got annoyed at Bonnie and she stormed off to her room and the atmosphere was still a little frosty between them this morning over breakfast. While parents and their children clashing heads is nothing new, I have emphasised to my husband several times that I want these last few months that our daughter is here to be perfect. Or at least as perfect as they can be. That means no picking fights over silly things and, as far as I'm concerned, arguing about what somebody is watching on TV is a very silly thing to fall out over.

As I make my drink, I am still frustrated that Lachlan lost his temper over us watching the documentary. I get that it might have been a surprise to see his home village on television, and also to be reminded of a tragic case that is utterly unpleasant for everybody. He admitted as much in the bedroom just before we went to sleep, accepting that he did know Paisley after all, despite initially denying it when Bonnie asked him. One thing that my husband has always made clear to me during our relationship is that he did not enjoy his time growing up in Carn-field, which is why he left at the first opportunity, which for him was as soon as he finished school at sixteen. It's also why he has never been back, so I guess it is within his character to get annoyed at the mere mention of it. But he shouldn't have lost his temper with Bonnie, nor was there any need for him to be so cold to me as we lay in bed and drifted off to sleep last night. I tried to snuggle with him, but he wasn't interested, so I gave up in the end and rolled over, feeling slightly hurt at being snubbed, but figuring it was best to leave him to cool off. But the problem is, he didn't seem his normal self this morning, so I guess it's still playing on his mind as much as it is mine.

I think about texting him and asking him how his day is going so far but decide to enjoy my drink first. I've earned it after a busy morning. Taking a seat on the sofa, I turn on the TV and am about to do what I usually do, which is scroll around for something I can watch mindlessly for half an hour before getting back to my tasks. But then I think about the documentary and realise that I could watch another episode of it now.

I'm certainly intrigued to learn more about Paisley's case, as well as about Carnfield itself, because Lachlan has always told me so little. I could easily watch it now, while the house is empty, and my husband wouldn't even know. But Bonnie would want me to wait for her and she would be able to see that I was an episode ahead of where we left it when she comes to watch again. But will she watch again? Her father's behaviour might have put her off, so she may not try and risk angering him again. So I guess this might be my only chance to watch more, while Lachlan is busy elsewhere and it's safe for me to do this.

Without overthinking it any more, I press Play on Episode 2.

I sip my tea as I watch the recap of events in the first

episode, which mainly covered the finding of Paisley's body in the woods surrounding Carnfield and how shocking such a discovery was in a peaceful village in Scotland. She was found with injuries consistent with blows to the head from a heavy object, and a rock was discovered nearby with her blood on it, making that the presumed murder weapon. Not a traditional murder weapon then, like a gun or a knife. Instead, this was a rock, which seems much more brutal, even more inhumane than the other alternatives. Although it also suggests it was grabbed as a last-second decision, which it may well have been.

But nobody knows.

Nobody seems to know anything.

As the second episode begins, it seems this one is going to focus on possible killers, as it is aptly titled 'Suspects'.

I feel slightly bad watching this knowing my husband wouldn't approve, but then again, he has no qualms opening a second bottle of wine on a Saturday night when I don't approve of that, so I guess this is the same. But it's not really. While wine is his way of unwinding after a long week at work, I'm watching this not only because I'm unwinding, or curious about the case, but also because I feel I will learn more about my husband's past by doing so. I know he won't feature in this documentary – why would he? But I do get to see his village and learn about the people who lived there, and that's far more information than I've ever got in all my years of marriage to the man who grew up there.

It feels mischievous of me to do this.

But a housewife has to get her excitement somewhere, right?

'As the residents in the village dealt with the shock, local police began their investigation and, initially, it focused on Paisley's boyfriend at the time, Angus Allan,' the narrator tells me. 'Also fifteen, he had been in a relationship with the victim for *several months prior to her death. On the night she is believed to have died, Paisley and Angus were seen walking through the village in the direction of the woods. The same woods where her body was found the following morning.'*

I'm utterly engrossed already, and the tea in my cup is growing cold as I keep watching. Who is this Angus Allan? Lachlan must have known him too.

'Angus was immediately taken in for questioning, but he denied harming Paisley and said that while he had been with her that night, he had left her in the woods and walked home alone. When questioned why he had left her there by herself on a cold, dark night, he had initially declined to answer, before eventually conceding that the pair had argued, and he had stormed off.'

I'm no detective but I feel the evidence is already looking bad for Angus. He was with her that night, they were in the woods where she died, and they argued. He's guilty as sin, surely? But there must be more to it because as this documentary revealed at the very beginning, nobody has ever been charged with Paisley's murder.

'As Angus was questioned further and forensic checks were conducted at the crime scene, many in the village had seemed to have already made their mind up that the guilty party had been caught. But when the rock covered in the victim's blood was forensically examined, none of Angus's fingerprints were on it. Nor was any of her blood on any of his clothes following a search of his items at his family home.'

I watch then as a couple of elderly residents are shown giving their thoughts on the news, though these residents must be long gone now, as they look to be in their eighties back in 2000. They seem to have made their mind up that it must have been Angus, which shows he was certainly tagged as the killer early on. But the forensic evidence seems to deny it. So what happened?

Did he do it or not?

Was the version of events he gave to the police the true version?

Or did he get away with murder?

Like the millions of people watching this documentary around the world, I cannot wait to try and find out.

SIX

LACHLAN

It's been a very dull morning at work, which has come as no surprise to me, a beleaguered office employee who has done this job for long enough to know that very rarely do fun things happen between the hours of 9 a.m. and 5 p.m. on a Monday to Friday. I analyse data for a large tech company, but lately, all I seem to have been doing is analysing my life and the results haven't been filling me with joy. But as I walk into the kitchen to get my lunch from the fridge, things brighten up slightly when I spot the person standing by the microwave.

'Hey, Francesca,' I say, smiling at my female colleague, who is looking radiant today in a bright dress.

Our office has a casual dress code and while I like it for the comfort it affords me in what I get to wear, I like it even more for what it allows the ladies in the office to wear. But don't get me wrong, I'm not some leering pig who forgets he's married. I appreciate a beautiful woman when I see one and I am certainly seeing one right now. The problem? The woman doesn't seem to be seeing me.

Francesca looks in my direction only briefly while replying with a half-hearted 'hey' before going back to what she was doing before I entered, which is texting on her phone while waiting for her lunch to finish cooking in the microwave.

I have to admit, her indifference to my appearance stings a little; it's a reminder of who I am now. No longer am I the youthful, attractive male that I was for many years. Rather, I am simply a man in his forties, and while I still consider myself to be handsome, I'm practically invisible to any woman in her twenties, as Francesca is.

I'm not going to let that stop me from trying to flirt with her though. The way I'm feeling, I could do with the ego boost, as well as the distraction from my job, my family life and that documentary that seems to have come out of the blue.

'You're looking nice today,' I say breezily before opening the fridge and reaching in for the tuna and cucumber sandwich Jenny made me this morning. 'I've just been in a meeting with Clive from accounts, and he didn't look quite so radiant.'

I chuckle at my own joke, the one at the expense of our colleague, Clive, who is a little on the large side and is prone to sweating during meetings even when the temperature isn't particularly high. If I was hoping that Francesca would laugh at my joke, thank me for the compliment and maybe give me one in return, I am disappointed because she doesn't do any of those things. She just lets out what can barely be described as a polite chuckle while keeping her eyes on her phone.

This isn't going particularly well. I am probably best quitting while I'm behind and taking my sandwich back to my desk, but I have one more go, eager to get some attention from the prettiest employee in the office.

'We haven't had any staff drinks for a while. What do you say we try and get something organised?' I suggest, wondering if the two of us could team up and arrange a social event for the rest of the workers here.

'Erm...' Francesca says while finishing typing her message, and when she lowers her phone and looks at me, the blank expression on her face tells me she wasn't even listening to what I just said. Before I can repeat myself, another colleague walks in. It's Rich, the twenty-eight-year-old software engineer with an annoyingly good head of hair and the kind of toned physique that I seemed to lose somewhere in my mid-thirties.

'Hey, guys,' he says coolly as he heads for the coffee machine. When Francesca sees him, she reacts totally differently to how she did when I walked in.

'Oh, hey, Rich! How's it going?' she asks him, stuffing her phone in her pocket, sticking a big smile on her face and seemingly ready to give him her full attention.

I don't need to be an expert in body language to see that she clearly has a crush on him, and I also don't need to be an expert to know that what interest she has in him is severely lacking when it comes to me.

Feeling unprepared, and unable, to try and compete against this younger man who is already several steps ahead of me, I cut my losses and leave the kitchen, arriving back at my desk with a sense of melancholy. Feeling invisible sucks, especially to someone I'm attracted to, but it's not a new feeling. I've experienced this a few times in the past, though I've learnt to handle my emotions differently.

Francesca is not Paisley.

She doesn't know how lucky she is.

Munching miserably on my sandwich, I plan to look at some football news online before getting back to work. Instead, I find myself scouring the internet in incognito mode for as much information as I can find about the new documentary that seems to have captured the interest of my wife and daughter.

After typing in 'Carnfield Paisley documentary' I get numerous results from websites all over the world. Wow, this documentary really has gone global. There are review sites here from as far afield as America and Australia, as well as plenty of news articles from closer to home talking about the documentary and bringing what was a very cold case back into the blinding spotlight.

I click on one of the links and start reading this review from a Scottish newspaper, which is obviously all over this, given their proximity to the case.

Streaming services did not even exist when the body of Paisley Hamilton was discovered on a grim morning in Carnfield, Scotland, on the fifth of September 2000. But the unsolved murder case is currently the most-watched documentary in several countries around the world, as viewers everywhere are gripped by the tragic tale of the fifteen-year-old and also the fact that, to date, her killer has never been caught.

I let out a deep sigh as I click another link.

A picturesque Scottish village and a gruesome murder seem to be the perfect cocktail of ingredients for true crime lovers all around the world, who are devouring every episode of a new documentary in which the killer remains at large, twenty-five years later.

My half-eaten sandwich is going untouched as I start to get a better picture of how big this documentary has become, and the more links I click, the more I read about the past. It's a past I've been running from for a long time, and a past that I never expected to threaten to catch up with me. But are things changing now?

ANALYSING THE PRIME SUSPECT IN THE PAISLEY HAMILTON CASE

I see the headline and scroll down for the article, and when I do, I see a photo of Angus as a teenage boy, the boy everyone thought was the one who had taken Paisley's life. He's in a very dated set of clothing, and the image seems grainy compared to the photo technology that exists today, but I can see the stunned expression on his face. It's the bewildered look of a youngster who cannot believe that he could go to prison for a crime he did not commit.

But Angus stayed free, as has everybody else who was living in that village at the time. The more I read, the more I am reassured that while everyone is speculating – from the documentary makers to the journalists and the viewers – nobody is any closer to catching the real culprit. If they only knew that the person they were looking for, the killer that seemingly everyone with a subscription to this streaming service wants to find, is the office worker who is about to throw his unfinished tuna sandwich in the bin. The office worker who couldn't even get so much as a smile out of his attractive colleague just now. The office worker who is far more dangerous than the wedding ring on his finger and the family photo on his desk would suggest.

The office worker who doesn't have it in him to kill again?

As I watch Francesca walking back to her desk, flirting heavily with Rich as she goes, I wonder if I might have just found what I've been looking for. I've been feeling so down lately, but it's not a mid-life crisis. It's the misery that comes from missing the thing that made me feel most alive. Killing interests me, and judging by the viewing figures of this documentary, it interests a lot of other people too.

Maybe it's time I gave them all something else to speculate about.

Maybe it's time to see if I can get away with murder one more time.

SEVEN

JENNY

The ringing of my mobile phone tears my attention away from the TV screen and as I answer the call, I pause the documentary. It's an action that is probably long overdue, as I've watched two episodes now and if not for this interruption, I could conceivably have watched the entire thing. But my best friend is calling, and it's a welcome reminder that the world is carrying on while I've been whiling away the afternoon on the sofa.

'Hey, Kath. How are you?' I ask the woman I have been close with since school, a woman who helped support me on my wedding day and vice versa. I'd do anything for her if she ever asked and I know she'd do the same for me, though thankfully, there has never been a drama big enough in our lives that has put our friendship to the test.

'Hey. Just calling for a catch-up. It's been a while,' she says, which is true. 'What's new?'

'Oh, not much. You know, just running around after the family,' I say with a chuckle.

'I've told you; you need to relax more. They're old enough to look after themselves now.'

'Yeah, right. If I left home, everyone else would starve within three days.'

'Lachlan must be housetrained by now?'

'If by that, you mean he knows how to get himself a beer from the fridge then yes. Anything else, no chance.'

Kath laughs and makes a few jokes about her husband too but, while it's nice to chat, I am still looking at the paused documentary on the TV and wishing I could watch more. That's because the more I watched, the more fascinating it became.

After hearing all about Angus and how he was a suspect only for there to be no DNA evidence linking him to the crime, the documentary told how his parents' house was vandalised because everyone in the village thought he must be guilty. Crucially, the police did not think the same thing, and as Episode 2 finished, the revelation that the investigation moved on to a mystery man who might have been passing through the village as a tourist was mentioned. Apparently, it wasn't uncommon for tourists to pass through Carnfield on their way to Edinburgh, or further north into the Highlands. The episode revealed rumours of potential sightings of this man, but nobody had a name and, therefore, he had never been found.

Was he the killer? Had he visited the village, seen Paisley and struck, before leaving and getting away scot-free?

I so badly want to know what really happened, but I cannot do that unless I watch more. Except I'm stuck on the phone, though I realise that if I can't watch the documentary, I can do the next best thing and talk about it.

'Have you seen this new documentary that just came out?' I ask Kath.

'The one about the dead girl in Scotland,' she cries, clearly knowing exactly what I'm talking about. 'Oh my god, it's so good! Who do you think did it?'

I laugh at my friend's enthusiasm, and it should be no surprise to me that we are on the same wavelength.

'I don't know. I'm only up to the third episode.'

'Ooooh, so you've not got to the one about the parents yet,' Kath shrieks, and I'm guessing by her excitement that it is a good episode. 'You need to watch that one, then call me immediately, so we can discuss it. I won't give anything away apart from the dad might be hiding something!'

'What? No way!' I cry, wishing I could press Play now so I could find out what this latest theory is all about. I don't want to be rude and end the call before it's time, though, so I head into the kitchen to make another drink instead while Kath chatters on about another episode I haven't seen yet.

'I reckon someone in that village knows who did it,' she tells me. 'They have to.'

I realise then that she mustn't have made the connection that Lachlan was born in the very same village, because she hasn't mentioned it yet, so she's really going to lose her mind when I tell her.

'Guess what?' I say as I wait for the kettle to boil again. 'You'll never believe it, but that's where Lachlan grew up. And he knew Paisley.'

'You're kidding me!' Kath screams down the phone. 'Seriously? I knew he grew up in Scotland but I didn't remember the name of the village. What has he said about her? Does he have a clue who did it?'

'He's not said much, actually,' I admit. 'He's never really liked talking about his childhood, and he says Paisley's murder is another reason he hated that place.'

'But we need the gossip!' Kath demands. 'He must know something! I can't believe he knew her!'

'Yeah, it's a small world, isn't it?' I say, shaking my head in disbelief.

'I need to come to your place tonight and talk to Lachlan. I have so many questions!'

Kath might be joking but to be sure, I nip that idea in the bud quickly.

'No, he really doesn't like talking about that place,' I insist. 'In fact, he got quite annoyed that Bonnie and I were watching the documentary last night.'

'Annoyed? Why?'

'He doesn't think she should be watching those kinds of things.'

'She's seventeen.'

'I know.'

It's good to hear that my best friend doesn't think I was over-reacting when I got annoyed at Lachlan last night. Then again, she would always be on my side no matter what, I suppose.

'Oh my gosh, I almost forgot!' Kath says next. 'Guess what I heard this morning at spin class? You know Sally, the young one with the red hair? Her husband has been having an affair!'

'No way!' I cry, taking my turn to be shocked.

'Yes way. She caught him with someone from work. The cheek of it! Seriously, what is wrong with men?'

'They're all dogs,' I say sadly. 'Apart from our husbands, obviously.'

We both laugh then, content in the knowledge that neither of our partners has strayed. We have actually admitted to each other before that our worst nightmare would be infidelity, and the possibility of having to go through a divorce, especially with our kids involved. Could there be anything worse than that? That's why it is a huge relief that neither of us has ever had to endure such a thing.

I lucked out when I found Lachlan.

Before our conversation can continue with any more shocking revelations, I hear the sound of the front door opening. When I do, I glance at the clock and realise it is much later than I thought it was. It's almost four o'clock, which means Bonnie and William are home. Where has that time gone? I realise that

I lost it all watching the documentary and, suddenly, I realise that if Bonnie makes it to the TV before me, she is going to see what I have been doing without her while she was out.

'I've got to go. The kids are home,' I say, and Kath understands, so we say a quick goodbye and I end the call before leaving the kitchen, passing my son on the way who mumbles something to me about him being starving.

'There's food in the fridge,' I tell him while trying to find his sister. But I'm too late.

'What's this?' Bonnie cries, and I enter the living area to see her holding the remote control and pointing at the TV. 'You didn't wait for me!'

'Sorry, I haven't watched much!' I try, but my daughter is too smart for that.

'You're on episode three!' she says. 'I'm going back to where we left it last night.'

She presses a few buttons so that she can return to the place where she last saw it, which is fair enough, but as she does, I remember how unhappy Lachlan is about her watching this and feel like I should at least make an effort to remind her of that.

'Your father really doesn't like you watching things like this. Why don't we put something else on?' I try.

'No way! All my friends are talking about this documentary and I'm way behind them,' she tells me. 'And you can't tell me not to watch it when you've had it on all day!'

Bonnie has me beat there, so I give up and make do with checking the time. Lachlan isn't due home yet for another couple of hours so it should be fine.

By the time he does get back, I bet he's forgotten all about this silly documentary anyway.

He doesn't have to know...

EIGHT

LACHLAN

My hands are squeezing the steering wheel as various images keep passing through my mind.

Paisley. Her parents. Angus. And that awful village I left years ago.

But as my house comes into view, I have to do what I have always done and push thoughts of them away in order to be the law-abiding husband and father that my family thinks I am.

'Hey! How was your day?'

Jenny's question is a friendly, inviting one but the only thing I want to be welcomed by is a cold bottle of beer, not the opportunity to talk about how I spent all afternoon ruminating over both the documentary news online and Francesca's total rejection of me earlier.

'Yeah, fine,' I mutter as I kick off my shoes and toss my car key on the side table. 'How was yours?'

'Oh, it was normal. Got all the jobs done. I didn't really have time for anything else.'

'Thanks for that,' I reply, figuring I better show some gratitude for the fact my wife manages absolutely everything around here, so I don't have to.

'The kids are home,' Jenny tells me as I head for the kitchen in search of that elusive beer. 'William's in his room and Bonnie's—'

'Dad, please can we go to Carnfield and see where you grew up,' Bonnie says as she comes out of the living area and catches me passing by.

'What?'

'I really want to go and see your childhood village. We should have a family trip there. How about next weekend?'

Bonnie seems serious, but I know my daughter. There's always more to what she says than meets the eye.

'If this is about the documentary then we are not having this conversation,' I say as I carry on into the kitchen, my daughter and wife following behind.

'No, it's not. I think it would be nice to have one last holiday as a family before I go to university.'

'And you want to go to a tiny village in Scotland?'

'Yes,' Bonnie tries as I take out a beer and grit my teeth.

'Nope. Not happening,' I say before I pop the lid off and take a gulp.

'Why not?'

'Because the only reason you want to go is so you can tell all your friends that you have been to see where someone got murdered, and they'll think it's cool that your dad is connected to the documentary you are all watching.'

'No, that's not the reason at all,' Bonnie feigns, but I am too tired for this.

'Drop it. We're not going there. If you want a family holiday, we can book something. We can go to Spain, or Greece, or anywhere we want to go. But we're not going to Carnfield. Seriously, there's nothing there.'

'Urgh,' Bonnie moans before storming out of the room, but I don't care. I know I was right. I'm not returning to that place just so she can take lots of photos and send them to her friends. I realise this conversation might not be over when I see my wife staring at me from across the kitchen.

'What?' I ask before taking another glug of beer.

'Bonnie's right. It is weird that we have never been to see where you grew up,' Jenny says. 'The kids know all about my upbringing, but they know nothing about yours and when they show an interest, you shoot them down, the same way you've shot me down over the years whenever I've suggested it.'

'The kids only know about your upbringing because we're living in your hometown,' I remind her. 'So it's easier for you to point things out from your youth as we drive past them every day. Sorry for not living where I was born for my whole life, but we're miles away from where I grew up and, regardless of the distance, how many times do I have to say it? There is nothing to see or do in Carnfield, so there is no point going all that way to visit it.' I'm hoping that is the end of the matter, but Jenny is not moving.

'We're going,' she says then.

'What?'

'We're going to go to Carnfield. All of us. Bonnie wants one last family adventure before she goes to university, and I want one too. And I think, rather than go to some bland resort in Spain like we've done a dozen times before, we should go somewhere that has meaning to us. They want to see where their father grew up and I want to see where my husband started his life. If it's not important to you, it's important to us. So we are going.'

'What's all the shouting about?' William asks as he enters the kitchen and, at the same time, enters this shambles of a conversation.

Before I can answer him, Jenny chirps.

'We're going to Scotland,' she tells our son. 'We're going to see where your father grew up because we love him and we want to go.'

'Scotland? Great! Can we go and watch Celtic play while we're there?' William cries, his passion for football at least giving him a better reason for wanting to go compared to my wife and daughter.

But while he has just spoken, I cannot allow what Jenny said to go by unchecked.

'You and Bonnie wanting to go to Carnfield has got nothing to do with love for me,' I point out. 'You've all got a morbid fascination with that stupid documentary. You and seemingly everybody else in the world who hasn't got anything better to do than watch it. Have you considered Paisley's parents? Have you thought about how they might be feeling, seeing their daughter paraded around on TV for entertainment?'

'They approved of the documentary,' Jenny says, which she might think helps her argument but only serves to give away how much interest she has shown in the very thing I am lambasting her for.

'How many times do I have to tell you? I have no desire to ever go back to that place,' I cry, throwing my hands up and, in the process, accidentally spilling some of the beer from the bottle.

'Why not? What's the big deal?' Jenny presses on, not allowing this argument to die out even though our son is here now.

'This isn't a big deal,' I reply, hoping I don't appear nervous as I speak.

'Isn't it? You keep telling me you don't want to go there, but you never give a good reason beyond you not being happy there. Don't you think it's time to go back and exorcise whatever demons you have from your past?'

'Exorcise my demons? What are you going on about now?' I scoff as I start to wish I had worked late at the office and avoided this mess entirely.

'What's all the shouting about?' Bonnie asks as she walks

back in, and I'm now very outnumbered because her arrival is hardly going to help my case that we should stay well away from Carnfield.

'I think everybody needs to calm down and let's change the subject,' I suggest before looking around the kitchen to see if there is any hint of what might be made for our evening meal. A bit of food might be the welcome distraction we all need, but sadly, I cannot see anything.

'I'm going to order a takeaway,' Jenny says, which sounds good until she adds the last part. 'Then we're going to plan our trip to Scotland and we're not going to argue about it because we're a family and it will be fun.'

With that, she grabs a takeaway menu from a kitchen drawer and walks out of the room, quickly followed by our two hungry children who excitedly tell her what they want to order before she makes the call. That leaves me standing alone with a half-empty bottle of beer in my hand and one very big question running through my head.

How am I going to get out of this?

My whole family is set on going to Carnfield, and I can't see how I can dissuade them. But they don't know what a problem this is for me. While for them, it would be a simple holiday, for me, it would be committing the cardinal sin of any criminal.

I'd be returning to the scene of the crime.

And from what I hear, that never ends well.

NINE

LACHLAN

Twenty-Five Years Ago

I cannot wait to leave this place. I hate everything about it. The quiet. The solitude. The lack of interesting things to do. The expectation that I'll grow old and die here like everybody else does. But most of all, *I hate him*.

Angus. My best friend. The person I have been close with ever since our parents made us play together when we were babies. That's how it goes here. You're given best friends rather than getting to choose them because there simply aren't enough people to choose from. I was born four days before Angus and as we were two male babies in the village, and our parents knew each other like they knew everybody else in this tiny place, we were thrust together and told to like each other.

I guess it worked for the most part. Everybody needs a best friend growing up and I had Angus. I suppose he did make my childhood better than it would have been if he hadn't been around. We raced our bikes through the village all summer. We had sleepovers in each other's bedrooms on cold winter nights to watch movies and listen to music. And as our imaginations soared, we talked about leaving this village one day and getting to experience life somewhere more glamorous.

Eventually, after so many years of being frustrated kids stuck in this place under the watch of our parents, we were finally getting old enough to start making that dream a reality. Fifteen, independence within our grasp, school life ending soon and the limitless possibility of adulthood beckoning.

Then my best friend went and betrayed me.

I'm watching him now, though he has no idea that I'm here. I followed him tonight, on this chilly evening that already feels like winter is here even though summer has barely ended. I'm wearing my coat and a pair of gloves, but it's not the weather that is making me so miserable. I'm in a section of the woods that surround this village, standing behind a tree and peering through the gloomy night at the sight of him.

With her.

They're sitting on a fallen tree trunk, looking comfortable and not cold because it's still the tail end of summer and while the sun has set, the air is still warm. I hear her laughter, cutting through the silence out here. Something he just said to her must have been funny and Angus seems pleased that he has been able to make her laugh. He's laughing too, and why wouldn't he be? He's with her, the most beautiful girl in our school year, and considering how small our school year is, there aren't many other contenders.

I've had a crush on Paisley Hamilton for as long as I can remember. Not quite as long as I've known Angus, but that's only because I wasn't sent on playdates with her by our parents. But I wish I had been. Instead, I had to make do with being sat in the same classroom as her for five days a week, and as the school years went by, my fondness for her grew.

I used to stare at her during all the lessons, initially not sure why I was entranced by her, as I was so young, just aware that she was different to everybody else and therefore made me feel different. As I grew, I realised what it was, thanks to watching movies and seeing characters on TV going through exactly the same thing.

I was in love.

For me, as a young boy in a village where nothing exciting ever happened, it was everything. It was my reason for wanting to go to school, my reason for looking forward to leaving the house because I might see her around. It essentially became the only reason I could bear living in this place.

Nobody knew how I felt about Paisley. Nobody until the night when, during a sleepover at his parents' house when we were thirteen, I told Angus about the crush I had.

He initially laughed and teased me, but that was only because he was my best mate, or so I thought at the time. I regretted telling him at first, but he promised to keep it a secret and, to be fair to him, he has done that. As far as I know, he has never told anybody that I like Paisley. But he has done something else, something much worse than sharing my secret with somebody.

A few months ago, I saw him kissing her.

As bad as that sight was, things have only got worse since. Angus and Paisley are a couple now, or at least whatever a couple means at fifteen years old. They're not buying a house together or starting a family, none of that adult stuff: it's obviously way too soon for that. But they are kissing and holding hands and spending all their time together, and the longer it goes on, the more the pain in my heart is turning into anger.

I'm angry at my best friend. He has betrayed me. I confronted him about it almost as soon as I heard, demanding to know why he had pursued the girl he knew I liked so much. He just shrugged and said she liked him and not me and that was it. He looked so smug when he said it, like he had an advantage in life that I did not – sure, I was a good friend, but he could get the girl.

It was in that instant that I realised he wasn't truly a friend, not when he was choosing her over me. But while I was angry at him, I was also angry at her. How dare she opt for him. How dare she hold his hand and rest her head on his shoulder and put her lips on his. I should be that guy! It was my dream to be that guy and the only thing that has made so many years in this village bearable. But now they are together, laughing and surely soon to be kissing again, while I am stood here, on the outskirts, spying on them from behind this tree and growing more frustrated by the second.

And then it happens.

I watch as Angus leans in for a kiss and Paisley reciprocates.

Everything goes quiet, there's no sound of laughter or chatter between them now. They are just kissing, and I'm watching the entire thing even though it is tormenting me.

I could leave. Go home. Try and find something else to do. Although it's not as if there is anything better waiting for me there. My dad's drinking has been getting worse and he seems to have developed a cough that never stops, so I don't want to be around him. And Mum is miserable all the time, smoking like a chimney, and on the rare occasions she doesn't have a cigarette in her mouth, she tells me that I am not to leave here when I finish school because it's not fair on her after she has raised me all these years. She suspects that Dad doesn't have long left to live, and she is probably right given how unhealthy he is. Therefore, she doesn't want to be left alone and puts pressure on me to ensure that doesn't happen.

I hate the guilt she tries to make me have, as much as I hate the fact that Dad won't even share one of his beers with me, drinking them all himself, telling me that booze is bad yet having more than his fair share, which tells me there must be some benefit to it somewhere.

I hate my parents. I hate home. I hate this village. Most of all, I hate the two people kissing in front of me.

I think about disturbing them. I could make a noise or throw something in their direction. They don't have to see me. They only have to stop kissing. *Please, just stop kissing.* But I don't do anything and, because of that, they have no reason to stop.

That's until I see Angus move his hand under Paisley's blouse, suddenly causing her to pull away from him and remove his hand.

'What?' Angus asks, before quickly trying again.

'No,' Paisley tells him this time, and she gets up from the trunk and seems to be preparing to leave.

'Hey, come on!' Angus says, getting up too and taking her hand. I figure whatever temporary tiff they had is over and they'll go back to kissing any second now. But then Angus goes from being the smug, confident guy who got the girl to showing a very different side to himself.

'It's been months now,' he says, still with a grip on Paisley's hand. 'When are we going to have sex? I thought that's what we were here to do tonight.'

'What? No, I thought we were just hanging out,' she replies.

'That's all we ever do!' Angus moans, and he's getting very agitated, which seems strange because he is in the position I dream of being in, so why isn't he happier?

'I want to take it slow,' she tries again, but Angus only grows more frustrated.

'Why are you being so boring?' he says, and with that, he turns and storms away.

Where is he going?

'Angus!' Paisley calls after him, but he doesn't turn back, and suddenly, he's left her alone out here.

Except she's not really alone.

I consider what to do then. I think about stepping out and saying something. Maybe I could cheer her up. Make her laugh. Take things slow like Angus didn't want to. Except I'm too nervous, so I stay where I am, or at least I try to. But a twig snaps underneath my right foot, and having made such a loud noise, it easily attracts Paisley's attention. As she turns her head, I'm not quick enough at getting fully behind the tree and she spots me.

'Lachlan?'

Oh no.

I can't pretend that didn't happen, so I have no choice but to step out from my hiding place and fully reveal myself.

'Hey,' I say meekly.

'Oh my god. Were you spying on us?' Paisley cries, clearly disgusted at the thought of that.

'No,' I try, but how can it be anything but that?

'Is that why Angus got so mad at me? Were you here to watch me have sex with him? Oh my god, you two are sick!'

'Wait, no, that's not it!' I say as I rush towards her before she can leave. Thankfully, she pauses, allowing me to try and make this better.

'He didn't know I was here,' I admit.

'You expect me to believe that? You're best friends.'

'No, not anymore.'

'What?'

I decide that I've got nothing to lose now, so I might as well give her the truth.

'I've fallen out with him. We had that fight at school, remember? You're the reason why. It's because he's with you.'

'What?'

'I like you. He knew that because I told him when we were younger, but he didn't care. So we're not mates anymore.'

Paisley stares at me and it's hard to know what she is thinking, though I am hopeful she likes what I said now she knows my feelings for her.

'You like me?' she asks for clarity.

'Yeah,' I say, wishing I could be more confident, but I feel so nervous and awkward. But maybe my confidence will grow if she reciprocates.

'Whatever,' Paisley says then, scoffing as she turns to leave.

'Wait! Where are you going?' I ask, rushing after her.

'I'm going home. Get away from me, you weirdo,' she says, and as she looks back at me, I see the worst expression I've ever seen a person give me.

It's not the sly look of my mother as she tries to guilt me into never leaving her. Nor is it the angry look of my father when he's had too much to drink and starts bemoaning his life. It's not even the smug look of Angus when I confronted him over his new girlfriend. This is worse than all of them put together because this is the look Paisley is giving me.

She is looking at me like she would never be attracted to me in a million years.

I don't know what happens in that split-second that my brain registers the dismissive look, but the next thing I know, Paisley is lying on the ground and the skin on my right hand beneath my glove is stinging. I guess I just struck her, but before she can get up, I am looking for something to silence her panicked cries for help.

I see a rock, so I pick it up and then I bring it down hard onto her head.

Now Paisley is quiet.

Now I am the last one left in the woods.

TEN

JENNY

Present Day

Ordering a takeaway is usually a fun time for a family. Everybody gathers around, united by their desperation to satiate their hunger with a calorific treat that is different to the usual, more mundane offerings that make up a typical meal. Then, when the food arrives, everyone sits around and eats together, laughing, joking, talking with their mouths full and bonding over a simple, shared occasion.

That's the way it is supposed to go, anyway.

But not tonight.

While I did order a takeaway for my family, there was none of the laughing or joking or bonding that usually accompanies it. That's because my husband did not want to eat with us and after that fracture line through our family, William quickly decided he would take his food to his room, leaving only Bonnie and I to eat together before she left for her room too.

I'm annoyed at Lachlan for ruining what should have been a nice night, but even more annoyed that it seems to be for a very stupid reason. He's still not happy after I said we were going to take a trip to see where he grew up, but what a silly reason to ruin a family meal. He hasn't even eaten anything himself. He went out for a walk before the food arrived and he hasn't come back since. At least the kids have eaten well. William piled his plate high with all sorts of delicacies from our local Chinese restaurant, before carrying his plate to his room because he didn't want to watch 'whatever rubbish you guys are going to watch on TV'. I didn't have the energy to tell him to stay and eat with us, though I did have the energy to tell Bonnie not to put that documentary on again.

'No way. It has caused enough arguments in this house,' I told her before swiping the remote control from her hand. 'We're watching something else.'

'But Mum! All my friends are messaging about it, and I still haven't finished it!'

'I don't care. I'm not having your father come home and get angry about it again, so it's not going on,' I insisted, firmly putting my foot down, but that was only the cue for Bonnie to take her plate to her room, presumably to watch the documentary on the TV in there.

So much for spending precious time with her before she goes to university. Somehow, I've succeeded not only in making her isolate herself from me, but from everyone else too.

I've barely touched my food, my appetite lost as quickly as my family members made themselves scarce, but all of this starts with Lachlan. Why couldn't he just have been excited about the idea of a family adventure to Scotland? He's always moaning about how hard and boring his work is, so the chance to get away for a few days should surely have been a welcome one. I know I could use a break from the normal routine too, and I'd love to get planning the trip. But would that be a waste of time if Lachlan is so clearly against it?

I'm browsing the internet on my phone and looking for hotels, but rather than feel the excitement that usually accompanies such an act, I am hesitant. That's because I am looking for hotels in or around Carnfield, the village my husband really does not want to go back to.

Unsurprisingly, given how remote it is, there are not many options for accommodation in the village itself, though there is a room available above the village pub. I imagine it's very basic, and imagining is all I can do, as there isn't even a photo of the room on the website. The price is cheap, but would Lachlan want to stay in the village itself? Perhaps it's best if I find us somewhere outside, so we can go in and see it and then leave quickly, so I hold off making a reservation for now.

Checking the time, I see that it is past nine o'clock and my husband is still not home. I consider calling him or at least sending him a message to make sure he is okay, but then remind myself that I'm not in the wrong here. He overreacted, not us. I can't hear anything from the kids either, suggesting they are well settled in their bedrooms and probably won't reappear again this evening. I expect William is watching football or playing it on his video game console, while Bonnie is most likely racing through the last few episodes of the documentary.

It's silly, but I feel a little envious of her because she's getting to find out what happens. I wish I could watch it, but like I said to my daughter, it's not worth the risk of Lachlan coming in and seeing it on the TV. But he can't see what I am looking at on my phone, so I temporarily forget about hotel hunting and look for articles about Paisley Hamilton.

It feels foolish for a woman my age to be addicted to something as silly as a documentary. I'm not a teenager like my daughter, so I'd like to think I'm more in control of my impulses and fascinations. Yet here I am, just like Bonnie, eager to learn more about this unsolved murder case. Who did it? How have they got away with it for so long? And will this documentary's emergence create a breakthrough for the police?

I start reading an article about Angus, the first suspect and the one who people are talking online about today as if he must have been the killer and somehow got away with it. The journalist who has written this article has apparently gone to Carnfield to track Angus down and try to interview him, and from what he has written, he found him.

One of the people at the centre of the documentary currently taking the world by storm lives alone in a very modest terraced house in the same village where Paisley died. Angus Allan, now 40, resides in his childhood home, only leaving it to get supplies from the local convenience store. The owner there tells me he comes in every day to buy a bottle of whiskey and a packet of cigarettes before taking them back to the house he grew up in.

Hamish McLaughlin, the shop owner, told me that Angus never moved out of his parents' home, and when they passed away several years ago, he stayed, inheriting the property and whatever money they left behind. 'He comes in every day and buys the same things. He doesn't look well, barely talks to anyone and generally likes to be left alone.'

I attempted to speak to Angus as he made his way to the shop one afternoon, but he rejected my questions about the documentary and Paisley Hamilton, before pointing out that he had received no money from the documentary makers.

It's a sad tale of a man who seems to have been trapped in the past, and I would feel sorry for Angus if not for the fact that there is a chance that he is guilty and managed to get away with a very serious crime.

'How was the food?'

I look up at the sound of my husband's voice and am surprised to see him standing in the doorway.

'I didn't hear you come in,' I say, wondering how he was able to be so quiet.

'I didn't make much noise. I thought you might have gone to bed.'

'No, I was waiting up for you,' I say, putting my phone down. 'Are you okay?'

'Yeah,' Lachlan says quietly as he takes a seat beside me on the sofa, and I sense a vulnerability about him.

'What's wrong?' I ask him. 'Why is the mention of Carnfield so damaging to you?'

Lachlan lets out a deep sigh but doesn't speak, so I take a guess.

'Is it your parents?'

He looks at me then and I sense a deep wound there, so I might have been right. Then Lachlan accepts it.

'Yeah, that's it,' he says quietly.

I should have known it. I should have been more sensitive. Now I feel bad.

'Why don't you tell me about it? If we talk about it, it will help me understand and then—'

'I don't want to talk about it,' Lachlan says with a shake of the head.

'That's the trouble. You never want to talk about your childhood, or your parents, or that village. But don't you see, that's why me and the children are so interested in going there. Because we feel like it's the only way we'll ever get a sense of your life before we came into it.'

'It's really not that interesting,' Lachlan says, growing annoyed again. 'I told you all you needed to know years ago. My dad was an alcoholic, my mum was a chain-smoking guilt-tripper, and I left them and the village because I knew there was a better life for me elsewhere. And I was right. I have you, and the kids, and this house, and my career. I made it. So why on earth would I need to go back there?'

I suppose he makes a valid argument, but whatever pain he suffered in his past, be it from his parents or village life, has clearly not healed, so I suspect his way of dealing with his problems is not the best one.

'It could be therapeutic for you to go back,' I suggest then. 'It could allow you to accept that place rather than hating it every time it gets mentioned.'

'So you're saying I need therapy now?'

'No, what I'm saying is we are your family, and we love you and we will support you if we go back there and it's too hard for you. If it's that bad we can leave, but I have a feeling you'll be okay when we're there. Once we've been, me and the kids will stop talking about going and we never have to go again.'

I'm trying to make it sound as simple and pain-free as I can, and I think I've done a good job of it. Lachlan isn't arguing back anymore, anyway. He's gone very quiet, which then makes me feel a little guilty. But should I feel guilt for wanting to learn more about my husband's past? Why is it so bad that I wish to know more about his childhood, his upbringing, his surroundings? They are all things I've wanted to know about long before now but have never had the chance to because he's always shut it down.

I could leave it there for the night, but I have one more thing to mention.

'What do you know about Angus Allan?' I ask.

'Angus?'

'Yeah. Were you close to him when you were at school?'

Lachlan thinks for a second before shaking his head.

'Nah, he was just another kid on the playground. We had games of football together, but that's about it. Why?'

'Just wondering,' I say.

'The documentary,' Lachlan guesses right, rolling his eyes. 'I guess I must be the only person in the world who hasn't watched this yet.'

'It's different for you. You're closer to it,' I say, but Lachlan surprises me by what he says next.

'No. If you and Bonnie are so fascinated by it, I'm willing to watch it. I'm sure it won't tell me anything I don't know about what happened, but put it on and let's see.'

'What? Really?'

'Yeah,' Lachlan says, picking up the remote control for me and then looking for it on the TV.

I can't believe this. Maybe that walk really did my husband good. Or perhaps I have worked my magic and made him calm down and see sense. Whatever it is, he seems happier, and we are now about to watch the next episode of the documentary together.

It might not be such a big deal after all.

Maybe my husband is back to himself again.

ELEVEN

LACHLAN

As any married man knows, keeping your wife happy is the key to being happy yourself. That's why, after my walk last night, I made the effort to try and appease Jenny rather than argue with her. Her obsession with Carnfield, an obsession she shares with my daughter, was causing me to get overly emotional, yet that is not the best way for a person with secrets to behave. I have prided myself on always staying rational and calm, so after the walk, and a couple of pints at the local pub, I went back to my usual easy-going demeanour.

Angry, frustrated, unpredictable people are capable of doing crazy things like taking a life. But nobody suspects the placid, ordinary ones – people like me. I proved it by not arguing with Jenny when she again discussed the possibility of going to see where I grew up. I also did it when I said I was willing to watch the documentary with her. And I am proving it again now by my song choice on the radio as I drive Bonnie and William to college and school.

'Dad, this music sucks. Put something else on,' William groans from the backseat.

'Yeah, it's awful,' Bonnie agrees, reaching out for the dial on the dashboard because she is sitting beside me in the front and, therefore, has access to the music choices too.

She changes the radio station while I keep focused on the road ahead, a road that is filled with other cars – commuters and parents like me who are trying to get their kids to where they receive their education before racing to the workplace on time. To any of the drivers of the other vehicles that surround us, I must look like the perfect family man, dressed for work but dropping the kids off before so my wife doesn't have to do it. If only they knew the darkness that lurked beneath the surface of my utterly unremarkable appearance.

'This is better,' Bonnie says as a more modern song plays, but William is not a fan of this either, probably as he rarely agrees with his sibling. But Bonnie is not changing the station this time, though I wish she had when the song ends and the radio presenters start talking.

'*Now was it just me or was anybody else up late last night watching the documentary about the murder of Paisley Hamilton?*' a male presenter says before his excitable female co-host chips in.

'*I binged it all in one sitting. It's so shocking, isn't it?*' she yelps, far too energetic for this time in the morning, but then again, that is the prerequisite personality for a breakfast radio host.

'Not this again,' I mutter, but Bonnie shushes me, clearly wanting to listen.

'*It really is gripping stuff, and I cannot believe it's a true story. For those listening who don't know, this is about the murder of a young woman that has gone unsolved for twenty-five years.*'

'*Isn't it incredible that the killer has got away with it for so long? I wonder if they're still out there.*'

'*If they are, they have surely seen the documentary now because it's all anybody is talking about, and it just seems to be getting bigger and bigger. Did you know that the village where the murder took place has reported that dozens of tourists have been arriving each day to take photos and visit the crime scene in the woods?'*

'Wow, that's incredible! I suspect there are a lot of amateur sleuths out there who are desperate to try and solve this case, considering the police clearly haven't been able to do it.'

'You're right about that, and for those who can't visit the village, they are on social media talking about what they think happened there. There are TikToks, and Instagram stories, and Facebook groups, all dedicated to this now. It seems everybody is desperate to solve this crime, but so far, nobody knows who did it.'

'Dad, watch out!'

Bonnie's cries snap me out of my trance just in time for me to slam on the brakes before I hit the stationary car in front of us.

'How did you not see that?' William asks me, clearly as anxious as my daughter is that we were almost involved in an accident.

If I was to answer truthfully, I would have to tell my son that the reason I did not notice the vehicle in front of us had braked suddenly was because I was finding it hard to believe that the people on the radio were talking about the crime I committed. But I obviously can't do that, so I need to say something else.

'I can't concentrate with this noise on,' I say as I turn the radio off, which at least means I don't have to listen to anything more about the documentary.

'You drive worse than Mum,' William jokes then, and Bonnie laughs. I'm not finding this funny though and, as the traffic moves on again, I just want to be alone as quickly as possible. But I can't get that alone time until I reach my destination, so I'm stuck with my kids for a little longer yet and even though the radio is now off, it doesn't mean the discussion about who killed Paisley Hamilton is over.

'I saw this video on Instagram last night from a cop in America and he says that the dad definitely did it,' William says, but Bonnie doesn't seem to buy that theory.

'No way. Why would he kill his own daughter?'

'Because he was having an affair and she found out about it, so he had to silence her or risk losing his marriage.'

'So he killed his daughter to keep his wife?' Bonnie scoffs. 'That's ridiculous. Plus, there was no mention of any affair in the documentary.'

'That's only because the parents made sure it stayed out of it. That was their condition for agreeing to be interviewed in the documentary.'

'What are you talking about?' Bonnie says, shaking her head as if she knows everything about the case and isn't simply guessing like everybody else.

'Is that true, Dad? Was Paisley's dad having an affair?'

I look in the rear-view mirror and see my son staring straight back at me in the reflection, eager to know my thoughts on this. Bonnie turns her head to look at me as well and despite having no intention of doing so, I have been dragged back into another conversation about the murder.

'How would I know?' I say as I put my foot down and go through a traffic light that turned red two seconds ago, but I'm not delaying this journey any longer.

'Because you knew all these people,' William replies simply. 'So was Paisley's dad cheating on her mum and then she found out? I think it's possible.'

'I don't know, and I don't care,' I say. 'It's none of my business and it's none of your business either. That family deserve to be left alone, not be speculated about by strangers all over the world.'

'They agreed to the documentary to raise awareness of the

crime and try to get it solved,' Bonnie says, which is not helpful to my argument. 'So when are we going on this trip? I've already told my friends that we're going to the village, and they are so jealous.'

'Right, we're here. Have a good day,' I cry as I stop the car and unlock the doors, relieved that I can kick the kids out without further questioning.

'What would you do if you were one of the suspects?' Bonnie suddenly asks, and my blood turns cold as I register the question.

'Excuse me?'

'Loads of people in that village have been listed as possible suspects. So what if you were? You'd be famous now like everybody else in the documentary.'

'That's not going to happen. I left there a long time ago.'

'But only after she died. You were there when she was killed, right?'

'You two need to get going or you'll be late,' I say, ignoring my daughter's last statement. 'Now go. I'll see you at home tonight.'

Bonnie eventually leaves my car, and I'm waiting for William to go too so I can re-lock the doors and then mercifully have some time to myself. But while my daughter has left, I notice my son is lingering on the backseat.

'Hey, what's the hold-up?' I ask him before noticing that he is staring at someone out the window. I look to try and see who it is and when I do, I notice two girls in school uniform walking past who appear to be the same age as my son. Then I have some idea about why he might be reluctant to get out of the car.

'Which one of them do you like?' I ask him with a wry smile.

'What? Neither of them,' William tries, but he's not fooling me.

'There must be a reason why you don't want them to see

you getting out of your dad's car. I'm guessing that it isn't cool. So, which one is it?'

William hesitates before finally giving up.

'The one with the dark hair,' he says shyly, and I smile.

'What's her name?'

'Rebecca.'

'Okay, and does Rebecca know that you like her?'

'No.'

I nod, understanding the dilemma.

'Well, the first thing you need to do is tell her. That way, if she likes you too, you won't waste any more time.'

'What? I can't do that!' William cries, mortified at the idea of telling his crush how he feels, which is totally understandable, but if I'm giving him fatherly advice, I have to be honest with him.

'Would you rather she started dating one of your best mates instead?'

'No way!'

'Well, that might happen if you don't hurry up and make your move. And trust me, you do not want that to happen. There's nothing worse than seeing someone you like with someone you know.'

William is quiet, so I guess he's taking on board what I said. Either that or he presumes I can't possibly know his pain because, like most kids, he can't fathom that his father had a life like his at one time in the past.

'Okay, she's gone, so you can get out now,' I say, and William reluctantly opens the door and leaves the car. 'Remember what I said,' I call to him just before he closes the door, and then I watch him walking towards the school entrance, trailing behind his love interest, but there is no sign of him hurrying to catch her up and engage her in conversation.

I drive away, satisfied that I did my best to impart my hardgained wisdom on him, and it was certainly that, because despite trying to push images of them out of my mind, my thoughts are filled with the sight of Paisley kissing Angus.

I have told my son what to do so he hopefully never finds himself in the same position that I did on that night in the woods.

I love him, so I don't want him to get hurt.

I also don't want him to get hurt in case he reacts violently to the pain like I did.

I don't want him to end up like me.

I doubt he'd be as good at getting away with murdering his crush as I have been.

TWELVE

JENNY

After all the drama lately with Lachlan, the documentary, and the steadily increasing sense of sadness I feel as the days tick closer to Bonnie moving out of home, it feels good to get out of the house and see some familiar faces. Every Thursday morning for the past four years, I've met my closest friends at the park before we embark on a ninety-minute powerwalk, giving us a great chance to catch up on each other's lives before we round the meeting off with a coffee and a slice of cake in the park's café.

The weather is dry for this particular meet-up, which is a relief. However, we tend not to cancel these get-togethers when it rains because if we did that then we'd barely ever get a chance to do this. The north of England is not known for its sociable weather. That's why it's always a bonus when the sun is shining, and as I greet my companions in the park, it's lovely to see that everybody is here.

Well, everybody but the person who is no longer able to join us.

As I greet my bestie, Kath, and my other two life-long friends, Elaine and Sue, I feel the pang of sorrow I always do when the four of us get together. That's because there used to be five of us in this tight-knit circle.

We sadly became a four on the day our dear friend Teri passed away in her home.

She was the same age as us, which means she died young, far too young, just thirty-seven, which is no age at all, but it was the age when we lost her. As tragic as losing her was, it's a double tragedy because she was murdered by an intruder who has yet to be caught. She was found lying on the floor in her kitchen by her husband when he got home from work, and while he was initially suspected, he had an ironclad alibi of having been away on business for the past two days with colleagues and Teri had died during that time. So it was some intruder, a burglar who probably presumed the house was empty only to get a surprise when Teri interrupted them. Whatever happened, and whoever did it, she's gone, which means she isn't here to walk alongside us as we start off along the park path with the conversation already kicking in. She is also a reason why I've avoided true crime documentaries, particularly in these last few years. Losing someone close to me in such a horrific way has totally turned me off to wanting to see death and the destruction it leaves behind on my television at the end of a long day.

'How is everyone on this fine morning?' Kath asks, getting the ball rolling as she usually does because she's always been the natural leader of our friendship group.

'Urgh, tired. The kids have been hard work this week,' Sue groans.

'Tell me about it. My two seem to be getting grumpier by the day. I'd take having two toddlers over two teens, that's for sure,' Elaine sympathises.

'No, you wouldn't,' I laugh. 'I mean, sure it's hard when they get to this age, but I wouldn't go back to the sleepless nights and the tantrums. No way.'

'Teenage tantrums are way worse,' Kath chips in with them. 'At least they are cute when they're little and you could always pick them up if you had to. Now they just smell and could pick us up instead.'

We all laugh at that as we settle into our brisk pace and smile at a friendly dog walker who passes us by with his Labrador.

'Girls, please tell me you've been watching this new documentary about the murder in Scotland,' Sue suddenly asks.

'I love it!' Elaine cries before Kath reveals my connection to it after I told her on the phone the other day.

'Lachlan is from that same village,' Kath exclaims. 'He was living there when that poor girl was killed. Isn't that right, Jenny?'

Everyone looks at me then, and even though we are still walking, it feels like everything has stopped because I'm suddenly the centre of attention and I've never enjoyed that. I'm not Kath, and even poor Teri liked the spotlight, but not me. But everyone is hanging off my next words now.

'Yeah, that's right. He grew up in Carnfield,' I admit, and Elaine and Sue start shrieking, loving a juicy piece of gossip as much as they usually do.

'So he knows everyone in the documentary? He knew Paisley?' Sue asks, and I nod, while feeling bad that my husband is such a hot topic when he would hate to be such a thing.

'It was a long time ago, but yeah, she was in his school year. He knew Angus too, but they weren't very close.'

'So what does he think happened to Paisley?' Elaine asks. 'Who does he think killed her?'

I realise then that despite all the discussion and arguments about the documentary between me, Lachlan and Bonnie, I have never actually asked my husband for his opinion on who the elusive killer might be.

'He doesn't know,' I say, figuring that would be his answer if

I did ask him because no one knows, do they? 'If the police can't figure it out, I hardly think my husband is going to.'

Everyone laughs at my jovial put-down of my husband, but it's done in good spirits, and they know I'm only teasing him. They never miss a chance to tease their other halves either.

'So you've watched the documentary together?' Kath asks me.

'I started watching it with Bonnie, and Lachlan wasn't too happy about that.'

'Lachlan hasn't seen it?' Elaine queries.

'He's seen a bit of it. He begrudgingly watched some of it with me last night.'

'Isn't that weird?' Sue asks. 'Him not wanting to watch it? Imagine they made a documentary about where we grew up, we'd be tuning in on day one, right?'

'Is it? I don't think so. I guess it's interesting to us, but it's like a sad story from his past and he's tried to move on like many others from that time have.'

'Surely he'd be interested? Especially if he knows everyone involved. I sure would be,' Kath says. 'It's like if they made a documentary about Teri's death, even though it would be painful to watch, I would have to see it and hear what was being said.'

'Me too,' Elaine agrees.

'Maybe we should pitch it to the TV companies,' Sue suggests. 'I mean, Teri's death is similar to Paisley's.'

'It's nothing like it,' I have to counter. 'Paisley was found dead in the woods. Teri was in her own home.'

'Yeah, but it's still two women who were murdered without the killer being caught,' Kath adds, unhelpfully for my argument.

'Seriously, Teri's death should be turned into a documentary. It has all the same ingredients as the Paisley case,' Sue says, warming to her idea. 'Okay, she was older but it's still the unsolved death of an innocent female in a place where people don't usually die in strange circumstances.'

'It's totally different,' I repeat, surprised my friend thinks the cases are in any way similar. 'Also, I don't know if it's best for Teri's family to become the subjects of a documentary, and it would be up to them to decide, not anybody else.'

But I'm even more surprised by what Elaine says next.

'How weird is it that Lachlan has been in both places at the same time?'

I stop walking. 'What do you mean?' I ask, and the rest of the group stop walking too.

'I'm just saying, he was in Carnfield when Paisley died, and he was here when Teri died. What are the odds of being so close to two random deaths?'

'What are you getting at? That he had something to do with them?' I ask as we continue to pause our walk.

'No, of course not! That's not what I meant at all!' Elaine cries. 'I was just pointing out the connection. It's obviously a total coincidence, but I was only mentioning it.'

'I love a good coincidence,' Sue says as Elaine looks sheepish. 'It's bizarre how the world works, and we're all connected to something else in some weird way. Imagine how many people we have been in close proximity to in our lives who have done something terrible. We might have sat next to a murderer on the train once for all we know. My point is, maybe it's not that weird. Maybe we're all connected to a crime at some point in our lives, every one of us, whether we knew the person involved or lived close to where it happened.'

I'm not sure such an unsettling thought is helping things, but Sue goes on.

'If they do ever make a documentary on Teri's death, Lachlan should be in it. He could mention knowing Paisley too. Attract all the viewers from that documentary as well. Make it an even bigger show. He could be a celebrity. We all could be.'

It's obvious that my friends are getting very carried away with things. As we start walking again, I stay quiet as they continue to chat about their fantasies of a documentary being made in our hometown.

'Imagine if we could find out who the killer is after all this time,' Elaine cries. 'The sense of justice it would bring, never mind the fact we might be saving some other poor person who is yet to cross paths with the killer.'

'I've spent so many nights wishing I could do this one thing in Teri's memory,' Sue admits. 'I can't bring her back, but God, I'd love to catch the vermin who hurt her. Make Teri cheer for us, wherever she is now.'

Sue looks up to the sky then, presumably because that's where we all feel like heaven is and that's where we all like to think Teri is in death.

While my friends could be accused of being very excitable housewives with not much else in their lives to get excited about, there is heart behind their desire to raise awareness about Teri's death and find out exactly what happened in her house that awful day. I want to know too, just like I want to know what happened to Paisley. But sometimes, we have to accept that there will be things we never fully understand.

Some questions will always remain unanswered. Some deaths will go unexplained. And some murders will go unsolved.

Not even a mega-popular documentary can change that.

Can it?

THIRTEEN

LACHLAN

Ego is a dangerous thing. Some might say it is my biggest weakness and I would probably have to agree with them. Without ego, I never would have killed Paisley. Nor would I have killed Teri, one of my wife's best friends who rejected my advances and threatened to tell my wife about my inappropriate behaviour until I staged a break-in at her home and silenced her. And without ego, I wouldn't be staring across the office at my colleague, Francesca, and fantasising about taking her life after she so easily rejected my efforts at conversation only to transform into an excitable chatterbox when a younger male colleague appeared.

It's not that I think I'm the world's sexiest man and deserve to have any woman I desire. It's just that I feel that I am handsome, and that, along with my charm, manners and sense of humour, should be enough. When it came to seducing Jenny, it certainly was more than enough and, if anything, it was almost too easy. But nobody likes doing things that are easy all the time. Everyone enjoys a challenge every now and again and that's why, for me, the females who have shown no interest in me are the ones who have caused me to behave violently.

My wife might consider herself unlucky if she was ever to discover my true nature; she would be shocked she has ended up married to a dangerous man. But in reality, she is extremely lucky because if she had rejected me, she might not be alive now.

I know I have a problem. I know it's not normal to want to violently hurt any woman who makes me feel inferior or, worse, invisible. But another problem I have is that I cannot exactly go to a therapist and share my issues with them.

'Hi, doc. What's the matter, you ask? Well, the thing is, whenever I like a woman, I try to get closer to her, but if she rejects me, I lash out and kill her. Do you think you can fix me?'

Somehow, I don't think that would go down well.

I'm still staring at Francesca as I ponder my personality, observing the way her hair rests gently on her shoulders and how she seems effortlessly at ease. This is exactly how it felt when I was watching Paisley from afar, only to see Angus swoop in and make her his. It was also how I felt when I started to get increasingly attracted to Teri, only to have to sit on the sidelines at friendship gatherings, watching Teri's husband with his arm around her while she laughed at his jokes but never seemed to find mine anywhere near as funny. If only she had laughed more, and if only she hadn't recoiled in horror when I had told her that I had been thinking about sleeping with her, she would still be here now. But like Paisley, she rejected me and made me feel bad about myself. So now they are both gone.

Having been frustrated by the unnecessary distraction the documentary has brought to my life over the past couple of days, I'm feeling much happier dreaming up ways I could get away with murder again. If I was to kill Francesca, hypothetically speaking, how would I do it? And more importantly – the most crucial part – how would I get away with it?

Like any killer, I would need several things beyond a simple motive. I'd need the opportunity to strike, I'd need the means of murder, and I'd need an alibi just in case any police officer ever started to ask a few questions.

Starting with opportunity, I scratch my stubble as I watch Francesca chatting to our male co-worker and think about how I could get her alone to do this. Ideally, I'd find out where she lived, so maybe I could follow her home from work one night. Getting her address is half the battle, but it's an easy enough obstacle to overcome. Once I know where she is, I can watch her and determine a time when she is alone. There is no wedding ring on her finger, nor have I heard her discuss a boyfriend and, judging by how heavily she is flirting with our colleague, I'd say she is very much available. That means she probably lives alone, though I cannot rule out a potential flat-mate. But again, that's something I can easily ascertain by following her home and watching for a while. Assuming she is living by herself, all I would need to do is get into her residence and she would be all mine.

How would I kill her? Hit her over the head with a heavy object like I did with Paisley? Stab her with a kitchen knife like I did with Teri? Or some other way? Some new and exciting method I haven't tried yet? I never know when the last time I will take a life will be, so it's always fun to experiment.

I'm past the point of feeling bad about my desires. That would only waste time, lead to negative thoughts and cause me to reflect on my life when I was younger, and none of those are things I care to do. Of course, I'm not so warped as to not be aware that taking a life is a bad thing to do; it's just that I'm only being myself when I do it. It must be nice to not have this compulsion, this urge, to hurt those who show no interest in me romantically. I imagine life is much easier for those people. It's probably more boring too. I can't deny that it's exciting to plot how to get away with murder.

If the opportunity and the method are taken care of, all I need then is an alibi should I ever fall under suspicion. The obvious one would be that I was at home with my family when Francesca died, but I'd have to go out to kill her, so that wouldn't be true. I need a way in which I genuinely am supposed to be in a different location so nobody can question it.

Then I smile to myself because I think I have it.

Jenny wants us to take a trip to Scotland. I've been dead set against it, but maybe it's the perfect excuse I need to book some annual leave and get out of here for a few days. If I'm off work when Francesca dies, any police officer who might call by will only be interested in those who were with her that day, not elsewhere.

I get a sudden surge of excitement because it feels like this is something that could work. But then a big problem looms large in my mind, temporarily spoiling my fun.

If I'm in Scotland with my family, how can I kill Francesca here?

Maybe I could do it before I leave, somehow kill her early in the morning or maybe the night before and then head north with my family, ensuring I am many miles away by the time anyone knows a crime has been committed. It's unlikely I'll be connected to it then. But what would make my alibi even stronger would be if I had already seemingly left town while Francesca was still alive. That's an ironclad alibi. I can't be accused of murder if the victim died while I was miles away.

I continue to stroke my stubble as I watch Francesca, pondering the next potential problem. If I'm in Scotland, how do I kill her?

What if I had an excuse to come back, something that only my family knew about? As far as everyone else would think, I was in Scotland the entire time, but what if there is a way for me to come back and kill her and nobody beyond my closest loved ones even knows I was here? That's perfect. I just need an excuse to give to my wife as to why I have to come back during our holiday. That's surely preferable to trying to sneak away from my family in the night and returning before dawn, which I will keep as a Plan B if Plan A isn't possible.

Like any crime, it's going to take a lot more planning than simply throwing a few ideas around and seeing what sticks. I'll have to give this much more considered thought if I am to pull it off. But for now, I've made a start, and it has certainly helped pass the time during my workday. I've been watching Francesca for a while and plotting her demise the entire time and not a single other person in here could possibly know it. But what only makes my desire to punish Francesca even stronger is that in all this time, she has not once looked in my direction. It really is like I'm invisible to her, so utterly unremarkable that she doesn't even feel the temptation to glance in my direction at least once to see what I might be doing. One look from her, at least to tell me I exist in some small way in her world, and maybe my burning sense of rage would dissipate somewhat. But she's giving me nothing. It's such a contrast to how she can't take her eyes off Rich. But that's okay because I've been in this position before and I know how to handle it.

I know how to come out on top and ease my anger.

And pretty soon, I'll have figured out a way to get away with murder once again.

If that's not a productive day at the office, I don't know what is.

FOURTEEN

JENNY

'How about we go to Scotland next week?'

The question from my husband surprises me, not because he's only just got home from work and has barely said hello but because it's usually me prompting him about taking a trip there.

'Are you serious? You really want to go?'

'Yes, but with one compromise. I don't go back to the village. If you guys want to go and see it, go for it. But not me. You can leave me in Edinburgh for a few hours and I'll happily take part in a whiskey tour until you return.'

Lachlan approaches where I stand at the kitchen counter and wraps his arms around my waist before kissing my neck. I was busy stirring sauce in a pan but it's impossible not to welcome the distraction, and I enjoy the attention I'm getting – it's nice to get affection rather than an argument.

'Are you sure you don't want to come with us?' I try one more time as Lachlan nuzzles his head into my neck, and I wonder what's got him in the mood for being like this.

'I'm positive. I don't miss that place one bit. But you were right. My issues with where I grew up shouldn't stop you and the kids from going there if you really want to, so I think this can be the best of both worlds. We get our holiday in Scotland, the last one as the four of us before Bonnie embarks on her university adventure, you three get to go to Carnfield, and I get to drink some wonderfully expensive whiskey in some great pubs in Edinburgh before we all come back home as one happy family.'

That does sound like a decent compromise, and considering what a good mood my husband is in, I'd be a fool to try and push for more from him, so I accept the suggestion.

'Okay, let's do it,' I say before turning around and giving him a kiss on the lips. 'How about I finish making dinner and then we can tell the kids while we eat?'

'How about I finish dinner, and you can have a glass of wine?' Lachlan says, smiling widely. I have to take a second to study his face and make sure he hasn't been swapped for another man. But it is really him, the man I married, and whatever I have done to deserve this pleasant start to the evening, I'll take it. So I leave him to stir the sauce that will accompany the chicken dish I have been preparing and go in search of that glass of wine I've just been 'ordered' to have.

As I pour myself a drink and Lachlan finishes making the food, I know I have lots to plan now for this little trip. Hotels, places to eat and drink, any sights worth seeing on the way – all that fun stuff, though there are also plenty of more mundane tasks to organise too, like mentioning to the neighbours that we'll be away for a few days so it would be kind of them if they could put our bins outside for collection in the meantime.

But the first job is a fun one – telling the kids that we are going on an adventure – and after calling them downstairs to let them know their meal is almost ready, I wait for them to take a seat at the dining table before breaking the good news.

'So, your father and I have decided that we are taking that trip to Scotland and we're thinking of going next week when the school holidays start. How does that sound?' I say, smiling, as I pick up my wine glass and catch the eye of my husband, who is smiling too.

'We're going to Carnfield? Brilliant!' Bonnie cries. 'My friends are going to be so jealous. Seriously, the photos and videos I can get there. I'll make the best TikToks!'

'No, you will not be disrespectful while there,' I reply firmly. 'A young woman died, and her loved ones still live there.'

'That's right. Don't be doing anything that draws attention to yourself,' Lachlan adds. 'I don't want to hear about anything bad when you guys come back to the hotel and tell me how it was.'

'Wait, you're not coming with us?' Bonnie asks, frowning.

'Nope. You three can go and I'll have a break from you all,' Lachlan chuckles as he pours himself his own glass of wine. 'I've seen enough of Carnfield to last me a lifetime and, trust me, once you've seen it too, you'll wonder why you were ever so excited about going in the first place.'

I watch my husband as he takes a sip of wine and think about how he is in a very jovial mood. But I also get the sense that there is more to it. He's being very jokey and light-hearted, almost like he's trying a little bit too hard, and even though it's nice to have him behave like this and not be grumpy, I wonder if he's only being so happy because he's figured out a way to appease us without doing the one thing he clearly wants to avoid.

Going back home.

'We'll drive up on the Thursday,' Lachlan says. 'I'll take two days off work and we can make a long weekend of it.'

'Wait, when would we come back?' William asks us then before we can all tuck into our meals.

'The Sunday,' I say, wondering why my son needs specifics, though I suspect it might have something to do with his social calendar. What else could there be for a fifteen-year-old to be worried about?

'I can't go,' he suddenly says, dampening the enthusiasm around the table somewhat.

'What do you mean you can't go?' I ask him.

'You'd rather stay at home than have a road trip?' Lachlan casually asks before another large swig of wine. He really does seem in a celebratory mood, though our son most definitely is not.

'It's the festival next Saturday,' he tells us then and, as soon as he says it, I do vaguely recall him mentioning a festival a while ago, though it's not like me to forget to put it on my family calendar.

'Next weekend? I thought it was later in the month,' I say, recalling the exact date now and relieved my 'mum memory' is not slipping after all.

'No, it's moved. It's next weekend and I can't miss it. Everyone is going,' William says. 'I'm not missing it. No way.'

'Nobody cares about a stupid festival for under sixteens,' Bonnie teases. 'It's not even a proper festival. There's no alcohol allowed there. It'll be boring.'

'Shut up!' William snaps, reaching across the table to try and make his sister regret mocking his social life, but as always, she ducks out of the way of his slaps.

'Could we rearrange?' I suggest to Lachlan, not wanting our son to miss what to us sounds like a fairly banal event but, to him, is probably the centre of his entire social circle.

'No, we're going next weekend,' Lachlan replies casually, as if he hasn't even considered it for a second, which is strange.

'No way! I'm not missing it!' William cries. 'You can go without me then. I'm staying here.'

'Haha, as if you think Mum and Dad will let you stay home alone.' Bonnie laughs. 'Good luck with that one.'

'Shut up!' William says again and, this time, he manages to catch his sister, slapping her on the arm and causing her to drop her fork.

'Get off me!' she cries and, suddenly, what started as a fun family evening is rapidly descending into chaos.

'Hey, calm down, both of you,' I say, trying to restore some order. I look back to Lachlan. 'I'm sure we could move the trip to the weekend after,' I suggest, but Lachlan still gives it little thought.

'No, it has to be next weekend. I've already booked the time off work and my colleagues have booked other days over summer, so this is the only time we can fit in a little trip before your sister's exam results.'

'You've already booked the days off?' I reply, astonished at how eager he is when he was resisting this trip all week. But annual leave can be quite competitive in his workplace, so maybe that's all there is to it.

'I'm not missing that festival,' William insists, standing up from the table and, while I try to get him to sit back down, he storms out of the room.

'So I guess we're not going to Scotland now,' Bonnie says with a sigh, and she sits back in her chair and looks like she's lost her appetite as quickly as William has.

'No, we are going. We're going next weekend and that's agreed,' Lachlan says, picking up his glass again.

'I think we need to rearrange. William really wants to go to that festival, and he'll be in a bad mood all weekend if he misses it,' I say.

'Then he won't miss it,' Lachlan replies with a shrug.

'What?'

'He can still go to the festival. I'll drive him back for it. We can leave Saturday morning, he can attend and then we'll drive back and rejoin you guys in the evening.'

I frown. That sounds like an awful lot of effort to make it work.

'You'd drive all that way and back again just for one day?

That's silly. It's over three hours each way,' I point out, but Lachlan seems to have it all figured out.

'No, it's actually perfect,' he says. 'While we are away, you guys can go to Carnfield and do whatever you want to do there. William's not as bothered about going as Bonnie is, so you two do that and we'll be back here and then we'll all meet up again afterwards for a nice evening meal and everyone will be happy. How does that sound?'

'Thank God we're still going! I've already told my friends I'll be there next weekend,' Bonnie says, relieved, and she starts eating again. Lachlan does too and I'm sure if he was to go upstairs and tell William that the festival was back on, our son would regain his appetite as well. But I've not regained my taste for the food yet. I'm trying to figure out why my husband seems dead set on us going away next week and not even a very long road trip with our son to make the festival is putting him off delaying it. He'd even booked the time off work before consulting with me.

What's got into him?

I guess I'll have to try and find out.

But in the meantime, I'd better prepare for our road trip.

FIFTEEN

LACHLAN

I can't say I'm thrilled to be on the road and back in the country I was glad to leave when I was younger. That's because I'm back in Scotland having crossed the border a while ago. I'm still over fifty miles away from the village where I killed Paisley, and I will ensure I continue to give it a wide berth, but I'm still much closer than I have been for a very long time, which makes me a little uneasy. I will be much happier when I'm coming back the other way, when I will be getting ever closer to Francesca, the woman whose life I plan to end next. It's all I've been thinking about lately, or at least it has when the subject of the irritating documentary hasn't crossed my mind.

Thanks to my son's attendance at an under-sixteens music festival, I have the perfect excuse to slip away from Scotland for a day and kill her without anyone but my family knowing I was anywhere near the crime scene. Everyone at work thinks I'm up north all weekend, so while they are all reeling from their colleague's death and the police are trying to figure out who did it, nobody would ever consider it could be me.

This is perfect. I was thinking I was going to have to make up some excuse to give to Jenny about why I needed to leave them for a while in Scotland, or otherwise risk sneaking away in the dead of night, but the festival is a gift-wrapped excuse that comes with the added bonus of making me look like the world's best dad. I'm making sure my wife and daughter get the holiday they want, while ensuring my son attends the social event he so desperately wants to be at, presumably because his school crush is going to be there too.

How considerate am I?

I'm at the wheel with my wife sitting beside me, while the kids are in the back, both of them with headphones on and engrossed in their mobile phones, which is making the start of this holiday a peaceful one. We left home two hours ago and crossed the border into Scotland just before midday, which meant we had made good time. However, we had a temporary delay not long after that, as Jenny wanted to get photos of us all beside the blue and white flag that was fluttering in the breeze high up on a flagpole in Gretna Green. Jenny wanted us to stop there not only because it marked the first step on our Scottish adventure but also because Gretna is a famous romantic destination, a place where young English couples would flock to when they wanted to get married before the age of twenty-one without parental consent. When Bonnie found out about that fact, she started filming videos, saying it was great content for her TikTok page, while William yawned and asked when we were going to get lunch. That was a good question and while we are back in the car now, as we want to get closer to Edinburgh, which is where we are staying tonight, Jenny and I are on the lookout for a suitable place to stop for food.

Then we see it.

'That looks okay?' Jenny says, pointing through the windscreen, and I look ahead to see an old pub by the roadside. 'Do you think they do food?'

'Worth a try,' I say as I steer us into the car park, and the sight of several other vehicles in here is a promising sign that we might be in luck.

As we disembark and head into the pub with rumbling stomachs and an eagerness to find a menu, I think about how this isn't so bad. Sure, I'm back in Scotland, but it's a big place and there's a lot of land to explore around Carnfield. I can have fun exploring that land with my family and leave that village well alone and everything will be okay. Jenny and Bonnie are set to go to the village on Saturday while I'm driving William back and forth to the festival and that's as close as I ever need to be to that part of my past. I'm not particularly nervous about my wife and daughter being there by themselves, even if I don't like the thought of them going into the woods where I killed Paisley. But as long as I don't have to retrace my steps with them then it's better than nothing, and this way, it kills the conversation about that place once and for all. This time next week, not only will my family stop pestering me about seeing where I grew up but there will be some other TV show taking the world by storm and that documentary will be quickly forgotten about, just like Paisley has been mostly forgotten about for the last twenty-five years.

'Thank you,' Jenny says as we take a seat at a table and a smiling Scotsman hands us our menus and asks if we would like to order some drinks.

William and Bonnie order their usuals, diet cola for her, full fat cola for him, before Jenny says she will have a glass of cranberry juice.

'I'll get an orange juice, please,' I say before looking down at my menu, but Jenny interrupts me.

'Why don't you get a beer? You deserve it after driving all morning.'

A refreshing pint of lager does sound good but it's not exactly the type of thing a person who has more driving to do should be drinking.

'I'd love to, but I can wait until we get to Edinburgh,' I say, thinking that will be the end of the matter. But apparently not.

'I'll do the driving. You enjoy a beer. This is your holiday too,' Jenny says to my surprise.

'You're happy to drive?' I ask, puzzled, because my wife is never usually eager to sit behind the wheel if I'm available to sit there instead. It's not that there's a difference between our driving abilities, just that she's always preferred to be the passenger.

'Yeah, I don't mind. These roads seem pretty quiet, and it'll give you a break. You've got this long drive to do all over again soon too.'

'It'll get busier as we get close to the city,' I try and warn her, but she doesn't seem worried about that.

'It's fine, seriously. You have a beer. I'm happy to drive.'

I'm not going to turn down the chance to relax a little and enjoy something a little stronger than an orange juice, nor miss the chance to switch off for the remaining ninety minutes we have left to drive to Edinburgh. Especially not when a beer or two will keep any nerves I have about being here at bay, as well as the nervous energy I feel for Saturday and what I will be doing to Francesca then. I won't be drinking that day because I'll need to keep a very clear head for what I will be doing, but we're not there yet, so I can indulge a little today.

'Okay, I'll have a beer, please,' I say triumphantly to the Scotsman taking our order, and Jenny looks pleased that I have accepted her invitation to get my own portion of this holiday started early.

Once our drinks arrive, I take a very satisfying sip from my glass, and by the time we have ordered food and it has been cooked and delivered to our table, I'm on my second beer. Jenny seems very keen for me to enjoy myself, and she and the kids seem to be having a good time too, judging by how much food they ordered. They go for dessert, though I decline a calorific snack in favour of one more drink. All that means is by the time the four of us leave the pub and are walking back to the car, our appetites have been more than satiated, and on top of that, I've got a bit of a beer buzz going on.

'Keys?' Jenny says to me as we reach the vehicle, so I pull them out from my pocket and hand them over, unable to resist making a joke as I do.

'Make sure you put your seatbelts on, guys. Mum's at the wheel now,' I say, and Bonnie and William are amused while my wife feigns hurt before we all get in.

As Jenny starts the engine and the youngsters on the back seat quickly stuff their headphones in their ears and lose themselves in their electronic devices again, I am basking so much in the warm glow of inebriation that I consider resting my head against the side of the window and closing my eyes. The urge to sleep is particularly strong as the sun breaks through the clouds, and the warm rays entering the car only make me even sleepier.

I decide I'll attempt to make the effort to stay awake in case Jenny needs help navigating us to Edinburgh, even though it should be fine with so many road signs along the way. But we've only been back on the road five minutes when the motion of the car causes my eyes to start feeling heavier and heavier.

It's okay, I'll just close them for a few minutes.

Like my wife said, this is my holiday too.

I'm going to make the most of it.

SIXTEEN

JENNY

When I suggested that Lachlan have a few beers with lunch and that I would drive us the rest of the way to Edinburgh, I genuinely did it out of nothing more than consideration for my husband and the desire for him to relax and unwind a little. How was I to know that he was going to fall asleep when we got back in the car and stay asleep almost the whole time I've been driving? I didn't want to wake him, and the kids were occupied, so I've driven on quietly, following the road signs and figuring that by the time we reach our destination, Lachlan will be well refreshed, and it'll be my turn to have a rest. But something happened along the way.

Things have changed, or rather, *the direction of this car has changed.*

Among the signs for Edinburgh, I saw one for a place with a very familiar name. The sign by the roadside told me that it was in a different direction to the capital city, so it wouldn't have made much sense to follow it, as it would have taken us further from where we needed to be rather than closer. But with Lachlan snoozing away beside me, I sensed an opportunity, and before my thoughts could talk me out of it, I made the turning.

Nobody knows yet but me. Not Bonnie or William because their eyes have been on their phones the whole time and certainly not Lachlan because his eyes have been closed the whole time.

Nobody knows that we are headed for Carnfield.

The slight pang of worry I feel is due to the fact that I told Lachlan he didn't have to go back there, so I am a little anxious as to how he will react when he wakes up and realises I have made a rather hasty decision. But he can't be that mad at me, can he? After all, my intentions are pure. I want us as a family to see where he grew up, so we should all be together when we go there, not split up. I am so eager for my burning curiosity about his upbringing to be quenched. And I have a feeling that when he is back in the village, he will realise that it's not quite as bad as he remembers it.

Another road sign tells me that we are five miles away from Carnfield now and despite us being well out in the country-side and surrounded by nothing but fields on either side, there is a steady stream of traffic going in the same direction as us. Either this route serves as a short-cut for local residents on their way elsewhere or the popularity of the documentary really has caused an increase in tourist interest around these parts.

As the road gets narrower and the traffic ahead slows, the change of pace must be the thing that stirs Lachlan from his slumber because he opens his eyes and gives them a rub before looking around.

'Wakey wakey, sleeping beauty,' I say, trying to keep things light and hoping I can delay him figuring out where we are for a few more minutes, as we are almost there. It would have been better if he hadn't woken until we were in the village, but then again, I wasn't even expecting an opportunity to get this close with him, so I should be glad I have made it this far. But there is the possibility that this turns out to be a very bad idea on my part, and as Lachlan tries to get his bearings, I anxiously await his verdict.

'How long was I asleep for?' he asks me.

'About an hour,' I say cheerily. 'You seemed very peaceful, so I didn't want to wake you.'

I figure I might as well throw that in so I sound like a caring partner, just in case his mood changes.

'Thanks,' he mutters as he rubs his face and stretches his arms before looking back at the kids, who still have their heads down over their screens. 'Everything been okay?'

'Yeah, it's been fine,' I reply, but surely Lachlan will realise we are not anywhere near the city soon... and then it happens.

'Wait a minute. Have you gone the wrong way?' he asks me, looking at the fields.

'The wrong way?' I reply, feigning confusion as Lachlan keeps looking around.

Then we both see it at the same time. The sign on the left side of the road up ahead.

The one that says

Welcome To Carnfield

'What the hell is going on?' Lachlan cries, and the volume of his voice is the thing that gets Bonnie and William to finally look up from their phones.

'Just calm down. It's okay. Let me explain,' I say quickly, figuring I can defuse his apparent anger. 'I was driving us to Edinburgh as planned, but then I saw the sign for here and thought it was a shame that we weren't all going together when it was so near. You were asleep so I made the decision to turn off the main road and come this way. It's only a little detour. We can carry on to Edinburgh afterwards.'

'No. Stop. Turn around,' Lachlan says, looking visibly stressed.

'What? We're here now, I'm not turning around.' I laugh, assuming my husband is being melodramatic.

'Seriously, turn this car around now. I mean it, Jenny,' he says, his voice firm, and I realise he really does mean it. I get even further evidence of that a second later when he reaches over to the wheel as if trying to take control of it himself, which is a crazy thing to do when he's not the driver.

'Hey!' I cry as he grabs the wheel and tries to steer us towards an area by the road that appears large enough for us to make a 360-degree turn.

As the cars ahead of us continue on in a straight line, we suddenly veer off the road, but in my shock at the unexpected move from my husband, I try to take back control of the wheel and straighten us up.

'Let go!' I cry, but Lachlan genuinely will not release his grip, and I cannot believe he doesn't realise how dangerous it is to do such a stupid thing, especially when we have our children in the car with us.

'What's going on?' Bonnie shouts from the back.

Glancing up at the rear-view mirror, I see the wide eyes of both our children staring straight ahead as we continue to veer off the road. They look afraid, and then Bonnie screams, which only serves to focus my mind on fighting to keep my own hands on the wheel and reduce Lachlan's power on it. But a tug of war over such an important thing as the wheel directing a moving vehicle can only end badly, and I realise that fighting it is only putting us all in more danger, so I relinquish control and allow Lachlan to try and finish whatever he thinks he is doing. But my sudden letting go of the wheel when Lachlan was trying so hard to make it go the other way means the car turns even more sharply than he expected, sending us veering off the road. I lurch forward in my seat, only my seatbelt keeping me from hitting the dashboard. Going off road so suddenly and swapping the smooth tarmac for the uneven ground beside it causes the front left wheel to slam into a large rock. It makes a dreadful noise, but only then do we mercifully come to a stop.

'Oh my god, what just happened?' Bonnie cries after a brief moment of silence followed the sickening sound of the wheel impacting the rock.

I turn around to check that both of them are okay.

'I think so,' William says in a small voice.

I turn to my husband as the anger inside me rises up as quickly and dramatically as a volcano about to blow its top.

'Are you mad? What were you doing?' I scream at him. 'That was so dangerous! Are you stupid?'

Lachlan better have a really good explanation for the nonsensical thing he just did; but rather than explain himself to me and his children, he simply opens his door and gets out.

'Where are you going?' I cry before opening my own door and following him out and, as I do, I see that the car behind us has stopped, and the driver has got out to check if we are okay.

I wave to him to let him know that we are all fine, at least physically anyway, before looking back to Lachlan, seeing that he is crouching down beside the wheel that hit the rock. While I am certainly no mechanic, even I can tell that the wheel is damaged, and not only is the tyre flat, but the axle it sits in looks to have buckled slightly, which is certainly not a good sign and, I'm guessing, not a quick fix.

My gloomy prediction about the state of this car is confirmed when Lachlan gets back to his feet and kicks the wheel as if taking out his frustration on it will help matters somehow. But I don't care about the wheel, not anywhere near as much as I care that my family is safe, and because we are, I'm not bothered if this means a delay to our trip. I just want to know what possessed my husband to do such a stupid and unexpected thing.

'Are you going to tell me what that was all about?' I ask him, grabbing his arm and turning him to face me before he can lash out at the damaged car again. But as he looks at me, I don't see anger or annoyance or even a sheepish look that might suggest he is about to apologise for the stupid move he made.

I see something I was not expecting.

I see fear.

SEVENTEEN

LACHLAN

I cannot believe this has happened. I cannot believe my wife took a detour while I was asleep and, in my haste to correct her decision, we damaged the car and rendered it unroadworthy. But most of all, I cannot believe where I am now.

I cannot believe I am back in this village.

'This is a joke,' I mutter to my wife as we watch a mechanic inspect our stricken vehicle. 'This has to be a joke.'

My wife doesn't answer me, either because she's still mad at me trying to take the steering wheel from her or maybe she is worried about our entire trip being ruined if our car cannot be fixed quickly.

The person tasked with trying to get our car roadworthy again was called by the driver of the vehicle behind us, who got out to offer us assistance before saying he would call the village mechanic and get him to come take a look at the damaged wheel. I told him he didn't need to do that and that I could figure it out myself, but it was painfully obvious to all of us that this needed somebody with better knowledge of car parts than me, so after I wasted some time pretending to know what I was doing, the mechanic was eventually called. Now there is a man in oil-stained overalls looking at the car while I stand by the roadside with my family, and it's a man whose name I recognised when I saw it printed on the side of his van as it arrived.

Graham McAllister – Auto Repairs

I remember a Graham McAllister from school, and while he was much younger then, not looking anything like this bearded, slightly overweight petrolhead who stands before us now, it must be him. There can't be that many people in the village with the same name. I recall that he was always into motors at school, working on his dad's cars with him while the rest of us played football on the village green, so I guess he grew up and followed his passion. It makes me envious that his is a passion that is respected and valued in society. Everyone likes a handyman. Unfortunately, my passion always has to remain a secret, just like I'd have preferred to have kept this village and everyone in it a secret from my wife and children. But Graham doesn't know I'm the Lachlan Ferguson he went to school with, not only because I haven't given him my name yet, but because I've obviously changed a lot in appearance since I last saw him. I'm not the scrawny teenager I was back then. I now have facial hair, more inches on my hips and the lines on my forehead that suggest I've been through a few trying times. I just asked him to try and fix the car as quickly as he could and then we would be on our way, after we had paid him for his services, of course. But he's been working on the car for a lot longer than I expected, and while he has a new tyre with him that is seemingly ready to go, something is delaying him putting it on our car. Then he approaches us and tells us what that is.

'The wheel arch is damaged,' he says as he wipes his hands on a greasy rag, and I get a strong scent of petrol as he comes closer. 'I'm going to have to tow it to the garage and take a look at it there. I can't do it here by the roadside.'

'How long will that take?' I ask, the question laced with a potent mixture of impatience and dread.

'It'll be in for at least one night, maybe two, depending on how it goes when I get it to the garage,' Graham tells me, still with seemingly no idea that he is talking to an old schoolmate and not just some stupid tourist who can't drive properly.

'Can't you fix it today? Please, I don't care what it costs. We need our car back.'

'I'll need to check if I've got the right parts, and even if I have, it'll take several hours. Time's against you today, I'm afraid. By the time we get the car to the garage, I'll be closing for the day. So it will be tomorrow at least before I can properly start work on it.'

As I listen to his explanation, an old feeling of frustration runs through me. Hearing him talk about how he can't work longer than his set hours, even for more money, is indicative of the small village mindset I was so desperate to escape. A mechanic in a city would work longer hours and gladly take the money, but here, in this place, all anybody wants to do is finish early and go to the village pub.

I turn away from the mechanic and put my hands on my head, letting out a deep sigh because that's the politest thing I can do at this moment in time. I can hardly berate him. If he doesn't fix our car for us, who will?

As I step away, I hear Jenny telling him to do whatever he needs to do, and he assures her he will before he goes back to work. That leaves us by the roadside, so what now?

'We'll have to walk into the village and see if we can find a place to stay for the night,' I hear Jenny telling the kids.

'Wait? What? We're not staying here,' I tell her and them, just to make it clear.

'Where else are we going to stay?' Jenny replies with a cold look in her eyes that tells me she is still mad at me but is presumably holding in that anger while we are out in public.

'You heard the mechanic. It's not going to be a quick fix, so we have to stay nearby while he works on the car.'

'I told you I didn't want to come here. Why didn't you listen to me? Look at the mess you've caused now.'

'The mess *I've* caused? I'm not the one who drove us off the road!'

'But you are the one who drove us here when we were supposed to be going to Edinburgh!'

Whatever reluctance either of us had to get into a shouting match out here, in the presence of not only our children but the mechanic and any nosey drivers who pass us by the roadside, has been lost. Our voices are only getting louder, that is until Bonnie steps in.

'Hey! Stop shouting at each other. You're ruining this holiday!' she cries, and Jenny goes quiet then. But I don't.

'It's already ruined if we're here,' I say, throwing my hands up. 'There's literally nothing to do here. I told you that, but you didn't listen and now here we are, stuck in this place, probably for days, when we could have been in a city spoilt for choice for things to do.'

I'm trying to blame my frustration about being here on the fact that Edinburgh has more to offer than Carnfield. Rather that than be honest and say that I'm worried about being so close to where I killed Paisley, because I fear that I'll somehow become a suspect if I'm recognised and the sight of me suddenly jogs an old memory of that fateful night twenty-five years ago. But I'm also frustrated as this has most likely ruined my plans for Saturday, when I was supposed to be driving William back for the festival before paying Francesca a visit. I'm not the only one who has just realised their weekend has been ruined.

'How am I going to make the festival now?' William moans as he watches the mechanic making a phone call that is presumably to the nearest tow truck driver.

'Don't worry, I'll get you there,' I say defiantly, not allowing this to derail both of our future happiness, even though things look pretty bleak now.

Jenny shoots me a cold stare, probably because I've made a promise to my son that I'll struggle to keep, and she hates when I do that as she's usually the one who has to pick up the pieces. But it's done and I'm not giving up hope that I can be driving back to England on Saturday so that William, and me, can get what we want. I could hire a car if mine is still unroadworthy, but that could be a hassle in itself, not to mention unfamiliar, and considering what I am driving back home to do, I want to be in my comfort zone as much as possible.

But it does occur to me that maybe this is a sign from the universe, or at least some higher power, that I'm not meant to do what I was planning to do to Francesca. The thought of quitting while I was ahead has often occurred to me and maybe this is a sure sign that I should do that. Maybe I'm not destined to take another life and, if I do, that will be the thing that eventually sees all my previous crimes come to light. The problem with quitting while you're ahead is that you always feel like you could have done more, and quitting does not bring the excitement that carrying on often does. I've spent these last few days feeling the excitement building up inside of me as I contemplate Francesca and what I will do to her. If I give up on that now, what have I got to look forward to? A quiet few days here in this village before returning home to my mundane existence, having to watch Francesca flirting with everyone in the office but me.

No way. I'm not going to allow this setback to change my plans.

I will kill again.

But first, I have to re-enter the village where I killed for the first time.

EIGHTEEN

JENNY

I'm so mad at my husband that I can barely find the words to speak to him. I expect foolish and possibly even reckless behaviour from my two teenage children who don't know any better, and part of growing up is making mistakes. But I did not expect that kind of behaviour from my husband.

Grabbing the steering wheel and running us off the road?

What possesses a grown man to do that when his family is in the car?

It was a good job I was behind the wheel, as any witnesses saw that I was driving, so even if the police come and breathalyse us, they'll only be concerned about my results, not Lachlan's. That's a good thing because he had three beers at lunch, so he will be over the safe driving limit. I wonder if being inebriated was the catalyst for doing such a stupid thing, but there's no excuse for what he did and as soon as I am alone with him, I will be demanding proper answers. But I'm not alone with him yet. Bonnie and William are with us as we enter the village, our car on the back of a tow truck and heading for the mechanic's garage while we make the five-minute walk from the scene of the accident to the heart of Carnfield.

'This is the worst holiday ever,' William moans as he trudges behind me, all four of us walking in single file in case any cars pass us on the way into the village.

'Shut up. You'll ruin my video,' Bonnie tells him, and when I turn back to look at her, I see she has her phone out and it looks like she is trying to document her arrival into Carnfield. My daughter's addiction to her phone, and sharing as many details of her life as often as possible, is not unusual for her age, nor is it unusual that I worry about it. She's making a video for her friends, no doubt, as well as her social media followers, but it's not exactly the right time for it. Not when her brother is so frustrated about potentially missing the festival on Saturday, and I guess it's that frustration that causes him to swipe his sister's phone from her hand and ensure the video is ruined.

'Hey! Give it back!' Bonnie cries, trying to take back what is hers.

'Stop messing about!' Lachlan shouts then and his booming voice instantly gets them both to start behaving again.

He really shouted at them then, far louder than he usually does, and it's another sign that he is not being himself. Usually, a person wakes up happier after a nap, but not my husband. He seems to have been possessed ever since he woke up and found out where we are.

As we walk a little further, the village appears before us, though it's hardly a dramatic and spectacular sight when it occurs. Lachlan was right. There isn't much here. Just a few rows of stone terraces, and some other buildings which I guess are what provide the locals here with their daily needs. There's a small shop to buy groceries, as well as a church and a pub, ensuring both saints and sinners are well catered for, and of course, the mechanic's garage where our car is currently being unloaded from the tow truck. There are some other buildings a little further in the distance, more homes presumably, although

I do notice one has a large concrete space outside it and I figure that's the school playground.

It's quaint and quiet. A quintessential village. While it's lacking in the amenities of a modern city, it doesn't seem as bad as my husband made it out to be. But when I glance at him, it seems as if he is eyeing each one of these buildings with suspicion, as if he knows they are not as picturesque as they seem.

'I recognise this!' Bonnie declares as we move deeper into the village. 'The church was on the documentary. It's where Paisley's funeral was.'

'Keep your damn voice down,' Lachlan snarls at Bonnie, but while I don't appreciate his language or tone, I understand why he is anxious for our daughter to be more respectful. Paisley's parents will be around here somewhere, and they could overhear her.

'Let's try the pub,' I say, pointing towards the old stone building with the words *Carnfield Inn* emblazoned above the doorway. 'I read online that they have rooms.'

'We're not going in the pub, and we don't need a room for the night,' Lachlan replies. 'We're going to the garage to wait for our car to be fixed.'

'Didn't you listen to the mechanic? Our car's not going to be ready until at least tomorrow, if not Saturday. So we need somewhere to sleep until then. Unless you know of any other hotels around here?'

I gesture to the sparse surroundings, at the few buildings and the fields that stretch beyond them, making more of a point than I need to but I'm still angry at my husband.

'We can stay somewhere else if we have to. It doesn't have to be here,' he grumbles. 'We can get a taxi and go somewhere else.'

'Getting a taxi around here?' I reply, looking around the quiet street. I'd say that won't be easy. But I don't want to go anywhere else. We've been cooped up in a car all day. 'You go to the garage if you want to but we're going to the pub. Come on, guys,' I say to Bonnie and William, and both of them prefer to follow me rather than stay with their father. It's not a surprise, as there seems to be a dark cloud hanging over him and who wants to be in the company of a person like that?

'I'll go and speak to the mechanic,' Lachlan calls after us, but I don't bother turning around to acknowledge him, instead focusing on the pub, which is open for customers – the front door is ajar and I can see lights on inside.

I pull the heavy door open fully before having to stoop to go inside, even though I'm not tall, and this really feels like entering one of those types of buildings that has been around for centuries. It smells like one too, and as we enter the musty pub, I look around at the people who are already in here.

There are at least six tables, and I count four people sitting among them, all men, all over seventy, and all with a pint of ale within reaching distance. They are also all eyeing us with suspicion, as if they know we are not locals so must have some nefarious reason to be here.

This place could use some music because it's awfully quiet in here, but the silence is broken by a voice from the bar, at the opposite end of the room to the silent men at the tables.

'Good afternoon. Is it a drink you're after or food? Our kitchen doesn't open until five,' says the curly-haired woman behind the bar. She looks to be in her sixties and is at such apparent ease in these surroundings that I guess she has either been working here for an awfully long time or maybe owns the place.

'We're actually looking for a room,' I say as I approach the bar while Bonnie and William linger back, a little hesitant to be surrounded by so many strangers. 'We had a car accident just outside the village and the mechanic says we might be stuck here for a day or two.'

'Stuck here? That's charming,' scoffs one of the old men behind me.

'Oh, no. Sorry, I didn't mean it like that. This village is lovely,' I say, trying to make up for my faux pas.

'Our dad grew up here,' Bonnie adds, which I'm sure she said as a way to make us seem more endearing to these locals, but I almost wish she hadn't. I expect Lachlan would rather people didn't know he was back here. It doesn't sound like he has many friends in these parts, though I doubt he has any enemies either.

'What's your dad's name?' the man asks.

'Lachlan Ferguson,' William replies, and I look around at the faces of the drinkers in here to see if that name is recognised by any of them.

'Ahh, Lachlan has returned, has he?' another man says, stroking his chin. 'He left when he was practically still a boy.'

'So what brings him back?' another man asks.

'We wanted to see where he grew up,' I reply, deciding to omit the part where Lachlan told us several times that he had absolutely no desire to set foot in this village again because I've already offended these people once since I walked in here.

'There's not much to see.' The man laughs, and the others chuckle around him. 'So where is he?'

'He's at the garage with our car,' I reply before turning back to the lady behind the bar. I need to ask her more relevant questions, not answer them all day. 'Sorry, do you have a room we could stay in?' I ask her again.

'We do have a vacancy,' she says. 'But only one room. It'll be tight with four of you in there.'

'It's fine, we can make it work,' I say.

'Really?' William questions, but I ignore him.

'Please book us in. And then we'll get some food when the

kitchen opens,' I say, smiling at the lady and trying to make it obvious that even though we are tourists and clearly city-dwellers, we will do our best to fit in and contribute while we're here.

I know that can be said of me and my children.

But what of my husband?

NINETEEN

LACHLAN

'Seriously, I'm willing to pay whatever it takes for you to fix this car as quickly as possible,' I say again to the mechanic, repeating what I told him when we were by the roadside earlier. We're now standing in his garage and my car is in position ready to be worked on, but that doesn't mean I'm any closer to getting out of here.

'Like I told you, it's not an easy fix. It'll take some time. I need all day tomorrow, at least.'

'There's nothing I can do to speed this up? Name the price,' I ask in frustration, wondering if Graham, this person who has lived here his entire life, isn't holding out for me to name some particular amount of money that will make him miraculously work quicker.

'It's not about money; it's about the time it takes. I can't change that, so either you accept it and leave me to get on with the job or you pay to have your car towed elsewhere. But bearing in mind it's over twenty miles to the nearest garage, and it will cost you plenty before the repair work even begins.'

The thought does cross my mind that I could have my car towed and, that way, we could sit in with the tow-truck driver and get the hell out of here. But that would be a strange decision to make. It's not a practical, normal one, which worries me that it would draw attention to myself. The last thing I want is everybody gossiping about the guy who was so desperate to get out of the village that he paid way too much money to do so, especially if they find out I used to live here. That does not seem like the behaviour of a person who has nothing to hide.

'Fine, please, work as quickly as you can,' I say before giving up and leaving the garage.

As I step outside, the sun that was poking through the clouds instantly goes back behind cover again and a coolness comes over me, as well as casting a huge shadow over the village. That seems apt, as if somebody is controlling the weather and toying with me, knowing how bad this place makes me feel and wanting the weather to reflect my mood.

I look towards the pub where my family will be and recognise that I should probably go and join up with them sooner rather than later. Even though I'm still mad at Jenny for bringing me here, and she's clearly still mad at me for causing the car accident, being with them has to beat being by myself. Just before I set off, though, I notice a couple walking up the road towards me. The second I do, I wish I was invisible, hoping to disappear like I'm a child playing a make-believe game about which superpower he wishes he could have the most. But this is real life, not superhero stuff, so of course I can't become invisible. That means I'm fully in the line of sight of the two people whose daughter I murdered twenty-five years ago in a spot not too far from where we stand now.

As I watch Mr and Mrs Hamilton approaching, their arms interlinked not only romantically but it almost looks like they are genuinely supporting one another to keep standing and plodding on, I note how they have aged since the last time I saw them in the flesh. I mean, anybody would age in two and a half decades, but these two seem to have done so even more. They're both only in their early sixties but they look well beyond that, each of them stooped, weary, walking slowly, seemingly lacking any energy or purpose other than to help the other one make it through the day. I don't know where they are going, and they don't seem in a rush to get there. It's almost as if they are filling the time between now and when they die, and probably, the only thing they really want to happen between this moment and that one is that they get some definitive answer about who killed their daughter.

They, like everybody else in this village, have no idea that I could give them that answer, but as they get closer, I feel the look on my face is about to give me away. I need to stop gawking at them and I need to untense my shoulders and not look so guilty. It's easier said than done, though, and this is exactly why criminals never return to the scene of the crime.

It's impossible to not feel like people can read your thoughts.

I've left it far too late to walk away now because this couple are almost upon me and I don't want to pique their curiosity by suddenly scarpering, so I remain where I am, frozen to the spot as they pass. When they do, Paisley's father looks up at me, and as we make eye contact and he stares into my soul, my heart is beating almost as quickly as it was on the night I took his precious child's life.

Is he going to recognise me?

Is he going to say something?

Is he going to accuse me of murdering his daughter?

Whatever is going on behind his tired eyes, I don't get an insight into it. He looks back down at the ground ahead of him and shuffles past with his wife, who doesn't raise her head at all to glance at me. I'm grateful for that, and as I watch them walking away, I am grateful that they didn't stop to talk. Even if they didn't recognise me, they could have asked me what brings me to the village and that would have been just as awkward to answer. Or they might even have accused me of being a morbid tourist who has come here after watching the documentary, and I doubt that would have been pleasant either. Best that no words were spoken between us. Hopefully, they never will be. With a bit of luck, I won't see them again for as long as I am here.

And then I realise where they are going.

They're about to enter the pub.

The same pub I have to go into to find my family.

TWENTY

JENNY

We're seated at a corner table in this small, old-fashioned pub, and we're sipping our drinks and looking at the food menus in preparation for the kitchen opening in thirty minutes' time. Even though my eyes are scanning over the limited but tasty-sounding options on this menu, my mind is on my husband and when it might be that he is going to come in here and join us.

I hear the door open then and look up, expecting to see Lachlan walking in, hoping he's apologetic and in a far better mood than he was when I last saw him. But it's not him I watch enter the pub, but two people I recognise from my TV screen at home – and I'm not the only one who recognises them.

'Mum, look who it is,' Bonnie says as she elbows me urgently in the ribs, causing me to squirm in my seat, though I do my best to not make too much of a scene and draw any attention to ourselves, and I really wish my daughter would do the same. We should not be gawking at Paisley's parents, who have just entered and approached the bar.

'Bonnie, settle down,' I say under my breath and, thankfully, my daughter is not lacking the awareness that this poor couple do not need anybody, let alone us, to make them feel even worse about things.

I watch as Paisley's parents get a drink at the bar from the woman who told us there was a vacancy here tonight before they take a seat at a table nearby. The other drinkers in here all raise their glasses to them, and one asks them how they have been, but I can't hear the response because Paisley's father talks in very low tones. As for Paisley's mum, she doesn't seem to be saying anything at all. She's barely even looking at anybody, which makes me wonder why she has bothered to come here if she doesn't want to socialise. Maybe she needs to warm up, or this is a better option than being sat at home with photos of her daughter on the wall to remind her of her loss.

My heart breaks for these two people, and while it did the same thing while I was watching the documentary, it's even more real now that I am only a few feet away. The TV screen could only do so much to convey their sense of loss, but now I'm in the same room as them, it's tangible, like their grief is emanating from every pore of their body and seeping out into those around them. Now, surely, we all feel too guilty about chatting about silly things and making a joke and, heaven forbid, actually laughing at something. Although I'm wrong about that because while I now feel very forlorn, and my children either side of me are just as quiet and pensive, the regulars in this pub are not.

One of the older men cracks a joke that causes everybody to laugh, and it's enough to raise a smile from Paisley's father, which looks to be just the thing he needed to raise his spirits slightly. Then the regulars carry on talking about what they were discussing before the couple entered the pub, and they also make sure to include them in the conversation and, as I watch them, I understand what is happening. The village residents are respectful of this couple's loss, but they are not treating them differently or doing anything to make them feel worse. They are talking to them like the neighbours that they are, normal members of the community, not the characters in a recent documentary that is being watched by total strangers all around the world, in far more exotic and busier places than this. It seems to be how Paisley's parents want it because they visibly relax. Paisley's mother actually speaks, making a comment on a church service that one of the older men here just referred to.

I realise I need to stop staring at the couple then so avert my eyes back to the menu, and when I notice Bonnie is still gawking too, it's my turn to give her a nudge in the ribs. She gets the hint and looks down at her own menu, and William is already doing the same, so I guess we can go on being fairly unnoticed and leave the long-suffering parents to enjoy their drink in peace. But as I hear the pub door open again, I have no choice but to look up, as I want to see if it is Lachlan this time – and it is.

My husband enters the pub sheepishly, as he should do because he still hasn't faced my full wrath yet, though I can't really be too expressive with him in such a public place as this. As he looks around, his eyes don't seem to land on his family sitting over here in the corner. Rather, they go to the poor couple who came in before him.

Of course he would recognise them and know what they have been through. I doubt they recognise him after all this time, he was just a boy when he left, and I get confirmation of that when they look up briefly at Lachlan before lowering their gaze back to their drinks. But Lachlan is still looking at them.

Why is he being so starey?

'Dad, over here,' William calls out, snapping my husband from whatever trance he was in, and he quickly makes his way over to us, taking a seat in the vacant chair. No sooner has he done that than somebody else in this pub tries to get his attention.

'Ahh, the wanderer returns,' one of the old men says.

Lachlan quickly realises he is talking to him. When he does, he looks at me, as if I've just given away his secret about him being from here.

'I told them,' William admits. 'They asked who we were.'

'Lachlan Ferguson,' the old man declares triumphantly. 'I remember you when you were a wee boy. Well, let's have a proper look at you then.'

The man approaches our table and, specifically, my husband, eyeing him up and down and apparently marvelling at how much he has grown and changed.

'Look at the size of you now,' the man goes on. 'Do you remember the time you stole a plant pot from my garden and when I chased after you, you threw it away and it broke?'

Lachlan looks guilty as charged and a little worried about what the man might say next. Bonnie and William just laugh, clearly enjoying hearing that their dad was as mischievous as them in his youth.

'You stole a plant pot?' Bonnie asks her father with a chuckle. 'Why would you do that?'

Lachlan doesn't seem to have an answer for that, but the victim of the theft does.

'Because he was a cheeky little troublemaker, like most of the kids his age were back then,' the man tells us. 'It's okay, there wasn't much else to do here, so you had to get your fun somehow. Don't worry, I forgave you long ago for your sins.'

The man puts his arm on Lachlan's shoulder, a friendly gesture. Though as he does, I notice my husband flinch and, bizarrely, for a split second, it seems like he is much weaker than the ageing man standing over him.

'So, you finally decided to come back and take a look around at the old place,' the man goes on. 'What do you think? It hasn't changed much, has it?'

'No, it hasn't,' Lachlan replies quietly.

'Do you recognise us all then?' the man asks, clearly happy

to make a big show of one of the old villagers returning. 'I'm not sure everyone recognises you. Guys, this is Lachlan Ferguson, and this is his lovely family. Let's make sure they have a wonderful time here. Who knows, they might decide to stay. We could do with the population boost, that's for sure.'

The man laughs at his own joke before giving Lachlan a hearty slap on the back and then finally returning to his seat, removing my husband from the spotlight, which is something that he seems very glad about. I watch Lachlan as he nervously glances around, and it's as if he's an anxious schoolboy on his first day in a new class where he doesn't know anybody. That's weird because really, he knows everybody here. They certainly seem to know him if the stolen plant pot story is anything to go by.

If the incident in the car didn't prove it, his demeanour now certainly does.

My husband really, really does not want to be here.

But why?

TWENTY-ONE

LACHLAN

Being here is torture.

Not physical torture like I'm in some medieval rack being stretched until my bones snap, but torture of the mental kind and, considering how I feel at the moment, the rack might be preferable.

'So, what other naughty things did you do as a kid?' Bonnie wants to know, looking at me while stuffing a chip into her mouth.

We've just received the meals we ordered. My family seem to be enjoying their food, but I've barely touched mine, although nobody around the table has commented on it yet.

'What?' I reply, my paranoid mind instantly feeling like my daughter is prying to reveal the worst thing I did here. It was certainly worse than stealing a local's plant pot.

'Did you steal anything else?' Bonnie goes on. 'I can't believe you were a little thief.'

She laughs, as does William, the pair of them enjoying the insight into my past that the old guy gave them. His name is Albert, and I do recall entering his garden and taking the plant pot. What he neglected to mention was that the day before, he had popped one of my footballs after it had gone onto his property, so my theft was simply retaliation for that. Two wrongs don't make a right, but considering what I went on to do not long after that incident, I'd say I was practically angelic at that time.

'No, I didn't steal anything else,' I say quietly before attempting to take a bite from my burger, even though my stomach feels sick, and I'd rather lie down in a dark, empty room. Instead, I'm here, in this pub, surrounded by people who knew me as a kid and, worst of all, with Paisley's parents nearby. It's as if I can feel their eyes burning into me over my shoulder. I want to keep turning around to check whether they are looking at me again or not, but I don't. If they are, I feel like they will know I am worried around them and then they'll start to figure out why.

I really could have done without anybody here knowing who I was, but that was not realistic, I suppose. Even if someone in my family hadn't told them, we'd have been asked. After all, this isn't the kind of place people randomly come to. They always have a reason. Maybe they got lost. Maybe they're here after watching the documentary. Or maybe, like me, they have returned to where they were born. There was no way I could be here without everyone realising who I was, which is why I wanted to ensure I never set foot here again. It's far too late for that now and after Jenny told me she has booked us a room for tonight, I won't be leaving anytime soon.

I hear the pub door creak open and instantly dread who else might be coming in here to make me feel worse. It's bound to be another person from my past, right? It turns out that I'm wrong because no sooner has the person walked in, they are being told to get out.

'Put your phone away before I break it!' comes the cry from

Albert, and I turn around to see a young man holding his phone up and seemingly either taking photos or recording a video. While that might not seem to warrant such a threat by itself, it's obvious why he is so keen to document this place. His camera is pointing at Paisley's parents, and he's saying something which I initially struggle to hear until it sounds like a narration of his visit here.

'Guys, I'm standing right in the heart of Carnfield, in the village pub that features in episode three, and guess what? Paisley's mum and dad are here!'

The young man is excitable, recording this video for whoever he intends to show it to, be it his friends or his followers, but it's clearly disrespectful. Within seconds, Albert is not the only one who wants this person to stop. Almost everyone in the pub, barring my family and Mr and Mrs Hamilton, rise up from their seats and head for the foolish young man, who quickly realises he is outnumbered and better leave promptly or his phone might not be the only thing that gets damaged.

As he scurries out of the pub, I get an insight into what life must be like for the locals ever since the documentary's release. Nobody here wants to be a celebrity and it's as down-to-earth and normal a place as one could find, yet this place is now famous. That doesn't mean the locals will tolerate rudeness though. The speed at which they sought to remove that man from the pub shows how they are willing to rally round and defend Paisley's parents and protect them from any more pain.

As everyone in the pub settles down again, Bonnie lowers her voice as she reflects on what just happened.

'That poor couple. They look so sad. If I was them, I would have moved away from here like Dad did.'

'This is their home,' Jenny replies, keeping her voice low too. 'And this is probably where they feel the closest to their daughter.'

'I know, but it must be so hard being surrounded by constant reminders. Surely it would be healthier if they were somewhere else. You know, to help them move on.'

'Maybe they don't want to move on,' William chimes in. 'Not until they've caught her killer.'

'I need another drink,' I say, breaking up this conversation as I get to my feet and drain the last of my pint. 'Anyone else want anything?'

Everyone still has most of their first drink left, highlighting how quickly I drank mine, so they all shake their heads, meaning I'm now going to the bar for only myself.

As I make my way to it, I'm forced to pass Paisley's parents, but I keep looking straight ahead to avoid eye contact with them until I reach the bar and set my empty glass down on it.

'One more of those, please,' I say, initially not recognising the woman serving me until I figure she is the daughter of the previous owner. I think her name is Charlotte, though I don't say anything. She doesn't seem overly interested in asking me about myself either, which I'm glad about, as I need a brief respite from the past. As she pours my pint, the pub door opens again and, for a place so small, I swear it feels like there's a constant churn of people coming in here. But it's no tourist this time. Rather, it's a local, and when I turn around and see him, I recognise him immediately.

His name is Gerard, and he was in my class at school. He used to sit at the desk behind me and would occasionally throw crumpled-up pieces of paper at me, just for fun, because class was boring. At break times, we would play football together or if it was raining, we'd hang around and whisper about which girls we fancied. I feel a wave of anxiety when I recall telling him once how I liked Paisley, but then most of the boys at school liked her, including Gerard, so I was hardly on my own there. Except we're not at school anymore. We're both here, standing in this pub and looking twenty-five years older, though I feel he has barely changed, and when he sees me, I get the impression the feeling is mutual.

'Lachlan?' he says, his eyes widening as if he cannot believe he came in here for a quiet pint only to bump into a long-lost friend.

I consider pretending like I don't know who he is, but that seems silly, especially when he's clearly not going to leave me alone to have a quiet drink now, so I welcome him too.

'Gerard? Wow, it's been a while,' I say, and I put my hand out to shake his.

He ignores it and pulls me in for a hug, and as he slaps my back, I feel like everyone in the pub must be watching us. It feels like it's impossible to not be the centre of attention here, and as we break off from the unexpected hug, I see everyone is looking, including my family.

'It's been more than a while! It's great to see you. I thought you'd never come back here again!' Gerard cries as the barmaid serves me my drink. He sees it and quickly declares that he will pay for it before ordering one for himself.

'I guess I haven't changed much if you recognise me,' I say with a nervous laugh.

'Changed? Of course you have! But I still recognise you. I looked at your sorry face every day in class for years, how can I forget it? You were as bored at school as I was. But look at you all grown up now. So, how have you been?'

'I'm fine,' I mumble back, almost feeling like I've been transported back to the classroom, not only because Gerard is here, but because there are so many people from the past.

'Are you here by yourself?' he asks as he looks around. His eyes land on my table in the corner and he figures it out.

'Is that your family?'

'Yeah,' I say, but before I can do anything else, Gerard slaps me on the back again before laughing and paying for our drinks. Then he carries his over to the table, and as he introduces himself to my wife and kids, I guess they're going to be learning even more about my past.

And there's nothing I can do about it.

Or is there?

TWENTY-TWO

JENNY

'Seriously, they don't want to hear all these old stories,' Lachlan says in a nervous manner as he interrupts his old school friend for the umpteenth time. But despite my husband suggesting that his family might be getting a little bored of some of the historical anecdotes Gerard has been spouting ever since he joined us at this table, he keeps going. No doubt it helps that the children are enjoying it too.

'Yes, we want to hear it all,' Bonnie says, relishing a chance to hear about her father's antics at school after so many years of him disciplining her for her own.

'Keep them coming,' William says for reinforcement, also motivated by a desire to get some measure of revenge on his father for all the times Lachlan has criticised him for getting a detention.

'Okay, let me think. What else did Lachlan get up to as a teenager?' Gerard says, racking his brains before taking another sip from his rapidly diminishing drink.

So far, this jovial Scotsman with a penchant for the past has told us about the time Lachlan instigated a fight during a football match against a school from another village, as well as when he and another pupil got caught throwing stones at the head-master's office window and were made to apologise in front of the whole school during the next morning's assembly. While it has been surprising to hear a few of the stories and discover that my husband was no angel as a teen, it's mostly harmless stuff. Many a school kid did a few things they shouldn't have while within the walls of education. Despite there not being any really shocking story to emerge, Lachlan has looked unhappy throughout this, mostly sitting quietly to the side and only speaking to try and get Gerard to stop reminiscing about the past. He's not had any luck with that yet, and it doesn't seem his luck will change as Gerard puts down his pint glass and prepares to launch into another tale.

'What about the fight you had with Angus Allan?' he says, looking at Lachlan. 'You must remember that?'

Lachlan doesn't say a word, but our daughter does.

'Angus Allan? He's the guy from the documentary, right?'

Gerard nods, not that I needed him to confirm that because I recognised the name from the documentary too, and more especially, that Angus was initially the prime suspect in Paisley's murder as he was dating her at the time of her death.

'Why did you fight him?' William asks his father, but he doesn't answer, allowing Gerard to step in again.

'That was the thing. We never found out. It was weird because you guys used to be best friends,' he says to Lachlan.

This is news to me.

Angus was Lachlan's best mate? He never told me that, even though I specifically asked him how close he was to that man. In fact, he told me he barely knew him.

'It was a proper fight,' Gerard goes on. 'I mean, there were always scuffles in the playground between the boys over some stupid thing. But this was a real fight. You were both going for it and had to be dragged apart.'

'What started it?' Bonnie asks, but Lachlan shrugs.

'Probably just a game of football that got a bit too competitive,' he says quietly. 'It was usually something like that.'

'No, that wasn't it,' Gerard corrects him. 'The fight started first thing in the morning as everyone was arriving for school. I don't know what caused it, but you two were really hitting each other. I guess that's why you stopped being friends...'

I observe Lachlan and figure he must know exactly what caused such a dramatic-sounding school fight. Although if he does know, he is not offering it up to us.

'It was probably over a girl,' Gerard says with a chuckle. 'Angus was popular with our female classmates back then. I was jealous of him for that, so I imagine you were too, as his best friend.'

'I don't really remember,' Lachlan says with a shake of the head, doing his best to look disinterested with this conversation. Except I can tell when my husband is acting, and I think he knows more than he is letting on.

'Anyway, whatever it was, I guess you had the last laugh,' Gerard says. 'I mean, here you are with your beautiful wife and two children, and Angus? Well, let's just say he's not done quite as well for himself since. I suppose that's understandable, given what happened...'

Gerard's voice trails off as he glances over at Paisley's parents, and I get that he is referring to Angus being a suspect in their daughter's death.

'Was this fight before or after Paisley's death?' I ask without taking much time to run the question internally, but blurting it out as soon as it comes to me.

'It was before,' Gerard replies. 'I know that because Angus didn't come back to school after he started getting questioned by the police.'

'Do you think he did it, Dad?' William asks his father.

'If the police don't know for sure, how am I supposed to?' Lachlan replies with yet another shrug, and his shoulders must be getting sore now considering how much he has done that since we came back to this village. For a man who has always had a brilliant memory and sharp mind since I've known him, there does seem to be a rather large gap in his memory when it comes to this place.

'What about you?' Bonnie says, looking at Gerard. 'Do you think Angus did it?'

Before Gerard can answer, I intervene.

'We shouldn't talk about this here,' I say, glancing over at Paisley's parents. While they can't hear our conversation, it seems wrong to debate their daughter's killer in their presence.

'Oh, don't worry about them,' Gerard says. 'Everyone in this village has a theory and everyone has told the parents about it at some point too. They don't mind, not when it's a local discussing it. It's just outsiders they aren't fond of. Lachlan is a local, so you guys are okay.'

'So, what's your theory?' I ask, now I have the green light to talk openly about this. 'Who do you think killed her?'

'This is why I didn't want to come back here,' Lachlan says suddenly, getting up from his seat. 'It overshadows everything about this damn place. I'm going to go and see if our room is ready.'

He heads to the bar then to ask the barmaid if we can access our room, but while he's gone, I look back to Gerard because he hasn't answered my question yet. Gerard is watching Lachlan.

'He is right,' Gerard confirms sadly. 'That murder ruined this place. Everyone here became less trusting after it. Some became bitter, especially Angus, which is fair enough if he is innocent. And a lot of people just became sad. I guess Lachlan was one of those. That's why he left.'

'You stayed,' I remind him. 'And you are a local, so you are entitled to have your opinion on it. So who do you think killed her?'

I wait for Gerard's answer while I see Lachlan talking to the barmaid, and then he turns and gestures for us to come to him, a strong hint that our room is ready, and we can go there now. But I don't get up, as I want to hear Gerard's theory.

He leans in across the table before giving it, making me think he doesn't want anyone else but us to hear it.

'I think the killer is in this pub right now,' he says shockingly. 'Or should I say, killers.'

'Who do you mean?' Bonnie whispers, leaning in herself, as does William.

'I mean,' Gerard says, his voice barely audible at all now. 'The couple over there, the grieving pair who have lost so much. What if they did it? What if they weren't happy with their daughter?'

'No way,' Bonnie says. 'It can't be them.'

'Maybe not,' Gerard says, sitting back again now. 'Maybe I'm wrong. Like I say, everyone's got a theory. Everyone who was here at the time. Like your husband.' Gerard looks at me. 'What's his theory? He's never actually told me. Has he told you?'

That's a good question and I can't answer it. Lachlan has never told me his thoughts on the murder. But as Gerard says, everyone here has one.

So what is his?

TWENTY-THREE

LACHLAN

Like everything in this village, the room we check into above the pub is claustrophobic, stifling and dreary. The décor is almost as dated as the buildings here, and the view from the window is as boring as the one I had as a child growing up, looking out over the main street and wishing I was born anywhere else in the world. It's the only place my family and I have to rest our heads until our car is fixed and it will have to do, though if it was up to me, we'd never be in this situation now.

'It's tiny,' William says, stating the obvious as he puts down the bags he helped me carry up the stairs. 'There's not even enough beds for us all.'

He's right there because while there is a double bed and a smaller single bed in the corner, they would only sleep three and we are a family of four.

'We'll figure it out,' I tell him as I look around. 'The girls can share the double bed, you go in the single and I'll make a bed on the floor. It's only for one night.'

I added the last part more out of hope than expectation, but I'm confident that a little positive or wishful thinking will make the mechanic miraculously work faster. Positive thinking has certainly been in short supply since I got here, but I am feeling a little better now I'm not sat in the pub surrounded by so many old faces. It's certainly nice to no longer have to hear Gerard telling my family all about my escapades at school, although not all of them were innocent and harmless examples of schoolboy shenanigans.

Why did he have to mention my fight with Angus? It was so unnecessary, as well as unnerving, because that fight preceded events that led to Paisley's death. While my family are never going to suspect me of killing Paisley, not unless something drastic happens at least, the other people in this village might, especially now I've popped back up again and re-entered their thoughts. I figured I'd been forgotten about here, barely a blip on anybody's radar, but now I'm back, it feels as if I'm the talk of the village.

I turn around as Jenny and Bonnie enter the room, the pair having trailed behind us so William and I had space to carry the luggage up.

'Not quite the holiday we envisioned,' I say to my wife as she looks around, but she doesn't seem too flustered about this being a potentially uncomfortable set-up.

'Why don't you guys go for a walk? I need to talk to your father,' she says to Bonnie and William.

I don't like the idea of her wanting to get me alone. Then again, I've done well to avoid it for this long, but I guess we're going to talk about the incident in the car now.

'I don't want to go for a walk. There's nothing here,' William grumbles, and I almost laugh at my son's very correct assessment of this place, but Jenny doesn't.

'Just go and get some fresh air. You'll be glad of it when you're back in here trying to get to sleep,' she says, and Bonnie needs less persuading.

'Let's go and explore,' she cries with her phone in her hand and an eagerness to presumably start taking photos to send back to her friends at home to show them she really is in the place where the documentary was filmed.

'Don't go too far,' I warn them. 'Stay away from the woods.'

That would be a normal warning for a parent to give their kids at the best of times when going out without an adult, never mind in a place where a terrible crime took place. But I say it as it creates the idea that the dangerous killer still lurks out there and, by doing that, it's creating a separation between me and them, even though we are really the same person. Of course, I'm not worried about them at all because I know there is no mystery killer lurking in the village. *Or at least not one who would hurt them.*

As Bonnie and William leave, their footsteps trundling down the staircase that takes them back to ground level, we're left up here, above the pub, and suddenly, this doesn't feel a better option than being back in the pub itself. As Jenny closes the door behind them and turns to look at me, I get a sense that I am right about that.

'You're going to tell me the truth and you're going to tell me now,' she says, instantly increasing my heart rate.

'The truth? About what?'

'About why you grabbed the steering wheel and made us crash.'

'I just didn't want to come back here,' I say for what feels like the millionth time. 'I admit it was a bad reaction and I shouldn't have done it. But we weren't going that fast, so it's not as if you and the kids were in serious danger. I'd never do that. You know I wouldn't.'

'No, I don't,' Jenny says, fixing me with a steely glare. 'I don't know because I thought I knew you, but maybe I'm wrong.'

'What are you talking about now?'

'I'm talking about all these stories of you at school. The trouble you got in.'

'Every kid gets in trouble at school. It's part of growing up,' I say, holding my hands out, as I can't believe she is having a go at me over this. 'Yes, I've done my fair share of troublemaking but so have our children and I dare say so did you too.'

'I never got into fights,' Jenny says. 'I certainly never got into a brawl with my best friend.'

I pause then because she is referring to Angus, so I might have to tread carefully now.

'Friends fight. Maybe you didn't throw punches, but boys are different to girls. We argue with our fists,' I say as casually as I can before picking up my bag and putting it on the bed as if I'm about to unpack. Of course, unpacking and settling in here is the last thing I want to do, but it's preferable to talking to my wife about this. Except she doesn't drop it.

'The thing is, you didn't tell me Angus was your best friend,' she says as I keep pretending to be busy with my bag. 'The person who was mentioned in the documentary as a prime suspect, and a person I asked you specifically about. You never once said he was your best friend. You said he was just some guy at school.'

'So what?' I cry. 'He's not been my best friend for decades. I haven't seen him since I was a kid. So he's not my best friend really, is he?'

'He was at one point in time, and you never mentioned it, like you never mentioned having a fight with him. Or any of the other things about your time here. I'm having to hear them all from other people, and even then, it's only because I drove you here while you were asleep. If I hadn't done that, I wouldn't know any of it, would I?'

'If you hadn't done that, we would still have a working car and we'd be in a nice hotel room in Edinburgh now, all of us with our own space instead of being here, cooped up in this tiny room,' I fire back mischievously, but it's also true.

'That's not my point and you know it,' Jenny snaps. 'My

point is that you are keeping things from me, and you are not telling me the truth. But not anymore. You tell me now. What is it about this place that caused you to drive our car off the road? What is in your past that I still don't know about? I'm guessing it's something that even Gerard can't tell me, or he would have done so already.'

'There isn't anything,' I try, but apparently, that's the wrong answer. Jenny picks up a pillow from the double bed and throws it at me.

It hits me harmlessly, not just because my wife doesn't possess a strong throw, but because the pillow is soft and thin and doesn't pack a punch, but it's the gesture more than the impact that matters. My wife is getting angrier with me by the second, and I'm not sure how I'm going to calm her down unless I come up with a better answer to her question.

'Either you tell me what it is, or we need a break,' Jenny says. 'I mean it. Unless you tell me what it is, you are moving out of our house for a while when we get back because I can't be around a liar.'

'Move out? You're seriously overreacting,' I tell her, but Jenny doesn't back down.

'No, I'm not. A person with nothing to hide doesn't run a car off the road. Only a person who is afraid does that. So what are you afraid of by being here? What is it that you were running from when you left?'

'This is ridiculous. I think I'm going to join the kids and go for a walk too,' I say as I head for the door, but Jenny steps in front of me before I can reach it.

'Is it something to do with Paisley?' she asks me as my blood turns cold.

'What?' I just about manage to utter while trying not to freak out that my wife has somehow figured out that I'm her killer.

'It is, isn't it? That explains why you got angry about the

documentary and also why you never talk about this place or wanted to come back here. It's because you know something.'

'I don't know what you mean,' I say, but Jenny keeps pushing.

'Do you know what happened to her? Did you see something?' she asks me. 'Do you know who the killer is and you're protecting them for some reason? Is it Angus? Did he do it and you haven't told anybody because you two were friends?'

I could breathe a sigh of relief because my wife hasn't come out and asked me if I am the killer, only if I might know who is. Although I can't relax yet as I still need to find something to say to get her to stop questioning me on this.

'No, I don't know who killed her,' I say, trying to make that clear before things escalate further there.

'Then what do you know?'

I desperately need a way for her to back off from me on this. Something. Anything. So I blurt out the first thing that comes to my mind.

'I don't know for sure. But if I had to guess, I think Angus did it,' I say quietly.

'Why? What do you know?'

'It was something he said once,' I say, doubling down on the lie that I'm going with. 'Before he was with Paisley. We were having a sleepover, and we'd just watched a horror movie about a serial killer.'

'What did he say?'

'He said he wondered what it would be like to take a life and asked me if I thought he could get away with it.'

Jenny's eyebrows rise as she processes that telling statement, which is utterly false, but she seems to be buying it.

'Oh my god. Have you told anyone else about this? Like the police?'

'No,' I say, shaking my head firmly.

'But you have to!'

'No, I don't. It's not proof of anything or an admission of guilt. Like I said, it was before Paisley died.'

'It's a pretty big hint and considering that she died while he was her boyfriend, I'd say there's a chance Angus did what he said to you. You think it too, right? You just said you think he is the killer, so you have to tell somebody.'

'No, I don't. I can do what I did when I was younger and stay quiet and, best of all, stay away from here. That way, I'm not putting myself in danger.'

'Is that why you left? You were scared of him?'

This seems to be going well so I nod to go along with that and, suddenly, Jenny totally softens, so much so that she moves towards me for a hug.

'Oh my goodness, you poor thing. You've been scared of him all this time,' she says as she squeezes me. 'That's why you didn't want to come back here. Because you don't want to see him. You should have just told me!'

I wish I had now: it's clearly a good excuse and maybe if I had thought of this lie earlier, Jenny would never have driven me here and I would never have had to steer us off the road. At least it's working for me now and I lean into the lie further.

'We need to try and avoid him while we're here,' I say. 'In fact, I think it's best if we try and avoid anybody.'

'Do you think we're in danger?' she asks. 'Oh my god, the kids. We need to go and find them. What if they bump into him?'

She lets go of me then and rushes to the door, but I stop her.

'No, stay calm. We don't act nervous around him if we do see him. He probably doesn't even remember telling me he wanted to kill someone, and I've gone all this time with no issue. We just need to lie low, get the car fixed and then get out of here.'

'And then we go to the police?' Jenny assumes, but I shake my head.

'No. Then we stay out of this. Promise me you will do that?'

Jenny looks at me and eventually she nods. But the action gives me a sense of unease. I'd hoped I was the only one lying throughout this conversation.

I think that has changed now.

I can tell she is lying to me too.

TWENTY-FOUR

JENNY

My husband's confession that he believes Angus is Paisley's killer might only have come about by me threatening to put our relationship on a break, but it does explain a lot of things. It explains why he left this village when he did, it explains why he never wanted to come back here, and it explains why he would rather fight me for control of a steering wheel than willingly arrive here as a passive passenger. He doesn't want to see Angus again, ever be around a person like him, a person who somehow, despite the initial investigation, has probably got away with murder.

I feel bad now for not only pushing my husband to the point where he panicked and crashed our car, but for dragging him back here in the first place. It's like me being taken back to somewhere I feel is dangerous, a place where a killer lurks and not only that but it's a killer who used to be my best friend. But there is a big difference between me and Lachlan.

I wouldn't have kept such a thing quiet from my partner like he kept it from me.

I also would have gone to the police with what I believed.

It's nighttime now and me and my family are all safely

tucked up in our beds. Bonnie is beside me in the double, William is in the single and Lachlan, as he volunteered to, has made a bed for himself on the floor. I think everyone is asleep as I can't hear any movement or voices, but I am very much wide awake. I'm still trying to figure out a way I can keep my promise to my husband.

I told him that I would stay out of the business with Angus, and Lachlan's suspicions of him, and do that by not going to the police and urging them to investigate that man again. Lachlan is probably right in his fear that the police won't be able to do anything with the news that Angus once pondered taking a life after watching a horror movie, but Angus would know Lachlan had spoken to them and then he could possibly come for him and us. The problem is, it doesn't feel right, not when there is a young woman who died, and justice is yet to be done for her and her parents.

I think about how fortunate I am to be lying here in bed beside my daughter, knowing she is safe and well. Compare that to Paisley's mother, who will never have that feeling again, and it doesn't seem right that Angus can continue to get away with what he did. I believe Lachlan and his feeling that Angus is the killer because he knew him extremely well. They were best friends, and friends, especially at that tender age, tend to tell each other everything and are not anywhere near as adept at hiding their real self as an adult might be. There's also the fact Lachlan had what sounds like a very serious fight with Angus, and while that was before Paisley's death, it's a sign that my husband was already beginning to turn away from him, perhaps sensing that Angus was trouble and cutting all ties with him.

After watching the documentary, I naively presumed Angus must have been innocent because the police investigation went nowhere. I even felt sorry for him at one point – how awful must it be for an innocent person to be accused of such a serious crime? Now I'm thinking Angus really is dangerous, and

I feel very differently about being here. Like my husband, I'm anxious and would rather be elsewhere, which is quite a dramatic turnaround from when I made the decision to come here in the car earlier today. It feels like I've blindly put my family in danger, and I wish we could just leave, a wish that will go unfulfilled until the mechanic tells us our car is ready to be driven again.

After Lachlan's admission that he felt Angus was dangerous, and knowing that man still lived in this village, I was eager to go and find Bonnie and William and bring them back to the hotel room before they potentially bumped into him. I didn't have to worry for long because they soon reappeared, looking miserable as they did.

'Dad's right. There really is nothing here,' William grumbled as he entered the bedroom.

'Yeah, it's pretty dead out there,' Bonnie said before laughing and acknowledging that she had made a pretty ironic pun.

'Told you,' Lachlan said, satisfied that his kids had seen what he saw in this place growing up, or rather, not seen.

'We'll go to the garage in the morning and check the progress on the car,' I said then, a plan for all my family to be aware of, but specifically my husband. It was my way of showing that I was back on his side and wanted to leave as quickly as he did.

As I lie here, I'm still wrestling with the concept of forgetting about Paisley and Angus and the fact that all this time is continuing to pass by without anything happening. I think one of the main reasons this is bugging me so much, besides the fact I'm a mother and can understand the pain of a parent, is also what happened with Teri. My friend's unsolved murder, and the helplessness I have felt about that, is making this harder to keep to myself because now I do have the chance to help. I wish I could bring Teri's killer to justice, but I can't as I have no clue who did it. I have a clue about Paisley, so maybe in some small way, it will alleviate the guilt I feel about not being able to help solve my late friend's case.

For now, I think the priority has to be getting the car fixed and getting out of here. Then, when we have some space, maybe I can talk to Lachlan about this again and see if he will reconsider going to the police and voicing his concerns. He could tell them that the conversation he had with Angus years ago had slipped his mind but coming back here revived the memory of it and that is why he is coming forward now. The police would buy that and better they do than think Lachlan sat on potentially useful information for twenty-five years.

I roll over in the bed, slowly and as quietly as possible so as not to disturb anyone else in this room, but as I change position, I catch a glimpse of my husband through the gloomy darkness. He is still awake because he's moving too, shuffling around on his makeshift bed, trying to get comfortable.

I want to say something to him, offer him some words or put my hand out and hold his, but I'll probably wake the others up if I do anything like that, so I just lie where I am and watch him. Lachlan eventually seems to settle down, and so do I, closing my eyes and doing my best to get some rest.

As I drift off, I see that I am no longer in the bedroom but out in the woods, seemingly on my own until I get the sense that somebody is watching me. I look around but can't see anyone, although I feel afraid, so I know I need to get out of here. But I don't know which way to go and the further I walk into the woods, the more lost I become. Then I see her. The woman covered in blood. Surely dead, yet she is standing and staring at me, her eyes wide open, pointing at something, or somebody, behind me.

She's trying to warn me that I'm in danger just like she was and while she has clearly been attacked, maybe there is still time for me if only I can get away. First, I have to turn around so I can assess the threat, so as I do, I expect to see him.

Paisley's killer.

Angus.

But the dangerous and deadly man approaching me is not Angus, though I do recognise him.

I know him all too well.

It's my husband.

TWENTY-FIVE

LACHLAN

I'm awoken by a loud thud, and the sudden noise, coupled with me opening my eyes in an unfamiliar place, causes a second of panic.

It turns out that the noise was caused by William accidentally rolling out of his single bed at dawn, and he woke us all up when he hit the floor and groaned. Once we'd all got over the shock of the sudden sound, and made sure that he was okay, we all laughed at his misfortune, and despite recent events, it was a fantastic way to release some tension. It was also a very good way of making sure we were all awake and out of the room early, which we are now as we head through the village towards the mechanic's garage.

It's only half past seven in the morning but the mechanic is at work, and when we enter the garage, I see our car where it was yesterday. That's not the only thing that is the same. The damaged part is still looking just as damaged too, which suggests we aren't going anywhere yet.

'Any progress?' I ask, more in hope than expectation, and the mechanic is initially baffled to see all four of us in his workplace as he looks up from underneath the damaged wheel arch.

'I'm still waiting on the spare part. It's not due in until this afternoon and I'll need a few hours to work on it, so it'll be tomorrow morning at best, as I warned you it might be at the start.'

'Is there no way you can do it quicker?' Jenny asks, as strong a sign as any that she is on the same page as me now, which is a huge relief because that should make my life easier.

'The part won't be delivered here until later today,' the mechanic repeats, looking irritated that he has to deal with two impatient people now instead of just me.

'Can't you go and collect it?' Jenny fires back.

'No, I have other things to do,' he replies with more than a hint of annoyance. 'I'm working as quickly as I can here, but you coming in isn't going to make it go any faster.'

'I knew it. I'm going to miss the festival,' William moans then, my son's disappointment at not getting to see his crush tomorrow written all over his frustrated face. But then...

'If the part is here by mid-afternoon, and I work late, I could have done it by opening time tomorrow,' the mechanic says.

'So we could be on the road this time tomorrow morning?' I ask for confirmation, and the mechanic nods.

'So we can still make the festival?' William asks, and I nod as it seems so – and that's not the only thing we could make. I could still see Francesca too, although after the regular bouts of guilt and anxiety I've felt since being back here, maybe I'd be better off not killing again.

Or maybe it's what I need to cheer myself up.

'We'll leave you to it,' I tell the mechanic before stepping out of the garage with my family following behind, and now all the four of us need to do is find a way to pass an entire day in this godforsaken place.

I'm considering suggesting a taxi again, but Jenny was right about that not being an easy thing to do around here. Besides, what if the driver turns out to be someone I knew from school and we end up sat in a car with another motormouth who wants to discuss my past as much as Gerard did last night?

'I better go and check if we can have the room again for tonight,' Jenny says, heading for the pub, and the kids go with her. I overhear Bonnie saying she wants a shower and William saying he might have a lie down because he didn't sleep well. That leaves me by myself, and I decide to take a quick walk around before I go back to the room and start going stir-crazy all over again.

I wander through the village, a task that doesn't take me long, and with every step I take, I am getting closer to the woods where I took Paisley's life. But I don't intend on going into them and I certainly don't plan on going back to the exact spot in the woods where she died.

'Good morning, old friend!'

I turn around and see Gerard heading towards me with a big smile on his face, and he's wearing a uniform that tells me he is employed in the local shop where the residents here can buy their groceries. I know that because the uniform has not changed at all since I was a kid and saw my mother wearing the same one as she went to and from work, a cigarette usually hanging from her mouth as she did.

'Hey,' I say, regretting not going back to the room with my family now, and I regret it even more when Gerard extends an invite my way.

'Me and some of the guys from school will be in the pub tonight. We meet every Friday in there,' he says as if there is anywhere else to meet around here. 'You should come along. They'd love to see you.'

I highly doubt any of them would love to see me, most probably because they've long ago moved on from the time we were friends. Then again, if they are still here, I guess they haven't moved on and I might be the type of entertainment they need to brighten their dreary lives. Either way, I don't intend to go and mix with even more people from the past while I'm here.

'Thanks, but I'm not sure if I'll still be here. The car might be fixed by then. If not, I'll probably have an early night.'

I hope that is enough to get Gerard to drop it and either talk about something else or better yet, walk on by and leave me alone.

'Mate, a word of warning while you're here,' he says, coming closer to me.

'What's that?' I ask nervously while looking around, but we are the only two people out here this early.

'It's Angus,' Gerard says as quietly as if we were surrounded by people.

'What about him?'

'He's never really recovered from the police investigation,' Gerard tells me. 'He started drinking a lot around that time and became quite reclusive. He stayed at home most days for years and when his mum got ill and passed, he just stayed in the house even more. He's still in there now and he only really ever comes out to buy more booze or, if he's really drunk, he goes into the pub and sits alone, cursing everybody under his breath.'

I instinctively look down towards the house at the end of the street because I know which property Angus lived in as a child and so I know where he must still be living now.

'Some days, when he comes out, he's okay. By that, I mean he's quiet. Keeps to himself. Just gets his whiskey and then goes back inside. But other days... it's like there's a darkness that follows him around and if he's really drunk, he can be trouble.'

'Trouble? What kind of trouble?'

'He gets angry. Abusive. He might start a fight. He thinks everyone here still suspects him and therefore hates him. He blames them for pointing him out to the police and making him suspect number one when Paisley was found.'

'He was her boyfriend,' I remind him. 'He was always going to be a suspect.'

'Doesn't change the fact that he maintains his innocence, so he feels like he went through hell having to try and prove it. And even though the police said they don't think it was him, mud sticks. He knows that everyone here has that question in their mind when they see him. *Did he do it?*'

'Why are you telling me this?' I ask as I keep looking at the house.

'I'm just saying, it'll be a surprise to him if he sees you, and if he happens to be in one of his bad moods, it might be dangerous. I mean, you guys fought before. It could happen again.'

'I'm sure it will be fine,' I say, though really, I have no assurance of that at all, and I hope that I don't have to see Angus and find out for real.

'It's just that everyone here has a theory about who killed Paisley,' Gerard goes on, and like when he was a schoolboy messing around in class, he never seems to know the right time to shut up. 'And... well... his theory involves you.'

'Excuse me?' I say, my breath almost catching in my throat as the words leave my mouth.

'Look, not many people know it because like I said, he keeps to himself and, most of the time, even when he does speak, he's blind drunk so people think it's just a load of gibberish. But I listened to him one night, a few years ago now. He was walking past the pub on a summer's evening, and he saw me having a beer. I waved to him, just to be friendly, and figured he would ignore me. But he didn't do that. He walked right up to me. And then he told me that he had been thinking back to that time when Paisley died.'

My heart is beating so hard in my chest that I'm amazed Gerard can't hear it.

'What about it?' I ask with great tension emitting from my every pore.

'He said the killer was one of the guys in our class who had a crush on her,' Gerard says.

'Like who?'

'Well, I mean, there were quite a few of us, weren't there?' Gerard says. 'But while I liked Paisley, I know I didn't kill her, and I know some of the other guys didn't either, as I was watching football with them at one of their parents' houses that night. But someone wasn't with us. Someone from our class who liked Paisley. You.'

I let out a nervous laugh and wait for Gerard to speak again. But he just stares at me, and I realise I have to come up with something quick to explain my whereabouts that evening.

'I was watching the same game myself at home,' I say, trying to relax. 'So it wasn't me either and if it was, do you think I'd come back here?'

'Hey, I'm not saying I think you did it,' Gerard says, putting his hands up by way of apology. 'I'm just saying that Angus thinks it could be you. It doesn't matter because no one would believe a word he says. He's the village drunk. Every good village needs one. Hopefully, it'll be me one day.'

Gerard laughs at his own joke before telling me he has to get to work.

'I'll see you in the pub tonight!' he shouts as he goes. 'Be there, everyone else will be. And who knows, maybe someone will have too much to drink and admit they're the one who killed Paisley.'

Gerard seems to enjoy his attempt at dark humour and chuckles to himself as he heads in the direction of the shop. But I'm not laughing and after watching him go, I look back towards the end of the street. When I do, I notice something different to the last time I looked. There is somebody at the window in the upstairs bedroom now, looking out, and I realise they are looking right back at me. Even from this distance, I know it's him and I guess he knows it's me.

Angus now knows I'm back in the village.

I just hope he keeps his theory to himself until I've had time to leave.

Otherwise, things could get very tricky for me.

TWENTY-SIX

JENNY

It's raining in the village, which has reduced our options of things to do even more. It's not as if we were spoilt for choice before, but thanks to the weather, even something as simple as going for a walk is hindered by the fact we'll be drenched if we spend more than two minutes outside. That means we really are struggling for ways to pass the time now.

Like many humans, when I'm bored I want to eat, which is why I have suggested a short trip to the village shop to get some snacks. Bonnie and William are keen, no surprise there, but Lachlan doesn't seem to have much of an appetite.

'This weather is horrible. Let's just stay inside,' he says as he gestures to the wet window and the numerous raindrops that are running down the outside of the glass.

'We have to eat something,' I remind him, not that he needs it because I heard his stomach rumbling earlier. It's no surprise as he hasn't eaten a thing since yesterday's evening meal. The kids and I had a very basic breakfast that was provided for us downstairs in the pub, but we need something more, so the shop it is and if we get a little wet on the way, so be it.

'We'll be right back,' I say to Lachlan as I leave the room

with Bonnie and William leading the way, their insatiable appetites fuelling their desire to get to our destination quickly.

When we step outside, the village seems deserted. It's not, of course, there are still people here, it's just that they are all inside, which is sensible, and like most places when the weather is rubbish, it's only the tourists who are foolish enough to go out.

We hurry down the street to the shop and when we get inside, I count three aisles stocked with all sorts of goods, from tinned foods to packaged meals. This place is actually bigger than I thought it would be. As Bonnie and William quickly go in search of crisps and chocolate, I turn down another aisle and no sooner have I done that than I see Gerard. He's wearing a uniform and stacking a shelf, and I guess that means he works here. When he sees me, he stops what he's doing and gives me a wave.

'How are you doing on this fine summer's day?' he asks me, and I smile at the joke.

'Not too bad, thanks. Just getting a few supplies. Our car should be fixed by the morning.'

'So you're still here tonight? Great, you can join us in the pub again! I saw Lachlan earlier and told him that several of us from school will be in there, so you should all come for a drink.'

My husband didn't mention that to me, so I presume that means he's not as keen about attending as Gerard is for us to do so, so I smile again to be polite.

'Yeah, maybe,' I say before picking up a basket and looking around at the goods for sale on either side of me.

'Let me know if there's anything you can't find,' Gerard offers. I thank him before moving on to the next aisle, thinking as I go about how nice he is and how content he seems to be here working in this modest place where he grew up. But I'm reminded that not everything is simple about this village life when the door to the shop swings open and I see Paisley's mother enter the store.

It's impossible for her not to catch me looking. I offer a smile but I feel like I should say something else to her, given how we are in such close proximity and are likely to bump into each other a couple more times before we have finished our shopping.

'Hi. I just want to say I'm terribly sorry about what happened to your daughter,' I lead with, figuring it's better to get to the point than dance around the elephant in the room and make small talk about the rain.

Mrs Hamilton takes a long beat before she speaks.

'Thank you,' she says before she picks up her own basket and starts adding a few items into it.

I figure I should get on with my own shopping, so I try to do that, but when I reach for a bottle of water at the same time as Paisley's mum does, I quickly pull my hand away and apologise.

'Sorry, you go first,' I say, on edge and fearful of getting in the way of this poor woman, as if she hasn't suffered enough and me accidentally picking up some grocery item she was going for will make her life intolerably worse. She must detect my awkwardness because she calls me out on it.

'Please, just relax. Everyone in the village walks on eggshells around me, but you don't need to. You're not from here. You don't know me or my husband and you didn't know my daughter. So you have nothing to be sorry for.'

She allows me to take the water I was initially going for. After I have placed it in my basket, she speaks again.

'While I wouldn't wish what has happened on anybody, it is comforting to know that nobody has forgotten my daughter,' she says. 'I'm guessing you saw the documentary.'

I nod.

'I just hope it does some good,' she goes on. 'But that'll only be the case if someone is brought to justice. I just hope I live long enough to see it.'

'Are you ill?' I ask, afraid that time might be running out for her faster than it should.

'No, but none of us are getting any younger, are we? Not me. Not you. And certainly not the killer.'

I initially hesitate to ask the question that comes to my mind then, but realise I might never get a better chance, so decide to go for it.

'Who do you think it is?' I ask, while being aware that Gerard is somewhere in the shop here and when I asked him the same thing, he suggested that Paisley's parents could be behind the terrible crime.

'I think it was somebody who knew her,' she replies, her grip on her basket as strong as the conviction in her voice. 'A friend. Somebody close to her. Someone who surprised her. My daughter was a very trusting soul. That trust was taken advantage of by somebody.'

'Angus?' I ask, but she shakes her head.

'I don't think he did it. You know why? Because he's still here. I reckon the real killer couldn't handle seeing me every day. That's why I think they left. Plenty of people have left this village over the years and not all of them have come back. I reckon the killer is well away from here and, if they have the good sense, they'll never come back. But maybe I'll get lucky one day and they'll return.'

With that, she places her own bottle of water into her basket and then moves on, continuing her shopping in peace, without further questions from me. Except what she just said to me means I am struggling to go back to my own shopping. I'm struck by a fleeting but terrible thought.

Paisley's mother, a person who knew her daughter better than anyone, has her instincts about the killer – and when are a mother's instincts ever wrong? That leads me to side more towards her theory, rather than Gerard's or anybody else's here.

She thinks the killer is someone who has left this village

since her daughter's death, and by the sounds of it, there are a few people who fall into that bracket.

My husband being one of them.

But she also believes the killer would have the good sense not to ever return to the scene of the crime, so that rules out my husband because he is back here, isn't he?

The thing is, he didn't come back of his own accord.

I made him.

TWENTY-SEVEN

LACHLAN

Jenny didn't tell me what was wrong when she got back from the shop, but I could sense there was something. She was off with me, and while she didn't hint at why, I could see the difference in her from before she left. I'm none the wiser as to what happened while she was out, and I haven't been able to discern much from Bonnie and William, who have spent the afternoon gorging themselves on snacks while staring at their phones with headphones in. I suppose that's a good way to kill a rainy day in a place like this, but while the kids have been fine, my wife and I have not.

Jenny has been very quiet, trying to take a nap at one point and otherwise, staring out of the window. I asked her if everything was okay. She just nodded and said yes before going back to her thoughts. As for my thoughts, they have been on the fact that if the car is fixed tomorrow and I get to drive William to the festival, I could get the chance to do the one thing that makes me feel worthy in this world. Francesca is on my mind and even though I know the risks involved if I try to kill again, I also know the risk of going the rest of my life wishing I'd done it when I had the chance.

I've been back in the village for a while now and despite a few uncomfortable moments, not least of which was Gerard telling me that Angus suspected me of killing Paisley, nothing bad has happened. Now there's just one quiet night to get through and I'll be out of here.

Easy.

At least that's what I thought.

'I guess we should start getting ready,' Jenny suddenly says just after six o'clock as I was contemplating closing my eyes and trying to have a very early night. The kids haven't heard her because their headphones are still in, but I caught it, which is why I'm frowning.

'Get ready for what?' I ask, puzzled.

'We're going to the pub tonight,' Jenny replies, getting up and heading for the bathroom. 'Gerard told me all your school friends are going to be there, but you already knew that. He told you too. So we better get ready so we don't miss them.'

'Wait, I thought we were staying in?' I protest. 'William and I have an early start tomorrow. We'll be on the road as soon as the car is fixed.'

'We don't have to stay up late,' Jenny says, pausing on her way to the bathroom to take some clothes from her suitcase. 'But we should go and say hello. I doubt we'll ever be back here again, so it'll be nice for you to see some old friends, won't it?'

Jenny gives me a forced smile before disappearing into the bathroom and locking the door behind her, and while that's her way of getting ready to go out, it's also a sneaky way of abruptly ending our conversation before I can dispute the idea even more.

I stand even less chance of that when she emerges from the bathroom and tells Bonnie and William that we are going downstairs to the pub for some food and drinks, because they don't need any persuading that such an idea offers far more fun than staying in here all evening. So, as my family get ready around me, I see only one way out of this.

'I can feel a headache coming on,' I say, feigning illness as I rub my temples. 'I don't think a busy pub will help, so I'm going to stay up here. Maybe I'll join you later.'

I wonder if such a cheap tactic will work, but I get my answer when Jenny looks at me like she doesn't believe me.

'Seriously? You're so desperate to get out of seeing old friends that you are faking a headache?' she says and then laughs. 'You're a worse actor than the kids when they wanted to get out of school.'

'Yeah, Dad. Even I could do better than that,' Bonnie says, and William also agrees that my acting needs some serious work.

Why does it feel like the longer I'm here, the less I'm able to manipulate them like I am used to doing at home?

As everyone is ready and heading for the door, I could either keep up with my feeble lie that no one is buying or grit my teeth and go downstairs with them and get this over with. Figuring that the worst that can happen is a few more awkward conversations with some familiar faces but nothing more than that, I decide to go down, comforting myself with the thought that I can at least get a warm meal in the pub to cheer me up.

But no sooner have I walked in than I realise my mistake in coming, because while I do see lots of old friends who all appear very happy to see me, I see one person at the other end of the bar who does not.

Angus is drinking in here tonight and judging by the look on his face when he sees me, he came out precisely because he thought he might bump into me.

As Jenny orders us some drinks and Bonnie and William look over at a group of teenagers who are making their way into the side room with a pool table in it, I do my best to not keep looking at Angus while people swarm around me.

'The traveller returns!' cries Duncan, the athletic guy who was always one of the best football players in our school year.

'You don't look a day over forty!' jests Craig, an old friend who often let me copy his homework after I'd failed to do mine.

'Why on earth would you ever come back to this place?' bellows Brian, always the loudest kid in class and now, seemingly, the loudest adult in the pub.

'I don't know. I guess home is where the heart is,' I say in answer to the question as I receive plenty of handshakes and backslaps and even more offers of a free pint of beer. 'Don't get too excited though,' I add. 'I'm not staying. This is just a passing visit.'

As everyone settles down and I get handed what is unlikely to be my last free drink of the evening, I glance over at Angus to gauge how much interest he is showing in me. To my relief, he's turned back to his own drink and isn't watching me, so maybe I can make it through the evening without having to exchange any words with him. I estimate that he is out of earshot too, though I'll keep my voice down as much as I can while speaking in here, just to be sure I'm not drawing even more attention than I already have.

I have to introduce Jenny, Bonnie and William to the group before my family take a seat and order some food. I catch up with my school friends while they wait for our meals to cook, hearing about all their lives now, although not many of them have done much beyond this village. Edinburgh is about as far as at least half of them have ever ventured. They all seem happy and that's the main thing. Everyone but Angus, who has been ordering several whiskeys in the time since I got here, and judging by how much he is drinking, I'd say he's either very drunk already or soon to be so.

When the food arrives, I temporarily leave the guys at the bar and eat with my family, and it's a relief to be away from them.

'Is it good to see everyone?' Jenny asks as I sit down. I shrug as I shove a chip into my mouth and say yes.

'Have you spoken to Angus yet?' is her next question.

'Erm. No,' I mumble before looking back over at him and, this time, he is looking at me. His eyes move from me to my wife, and finally, to my children, all while he sips his latest whiskey. He has bleary eyes, but I sense a disturbing focus behind them at the same time.

'Can we go and play pool?' Bonnie asks when she has finished her meal, and William seems keen to go with her, so I give them a couple of pound coins to pay for the table and watch them head away. The group of teenage guys is still in there, but I guess they'll wait their turn to play. But while I'm distracted watching them go, I fail to notice who has just sat down at our table until it is too late to stop them.

'Hello, old pal.'

The voice is slurred, but I still recognise it, like I still recognise the face, even though it's been aged somewhat by years of alcohol abuse and a lack of vitamin D. Angus is now sitting with me and Jenny, and judging by the sneer on his face, he hasn't come over simply to say hello.

'You must be Lachlan's wife,' Angus says, extending his hand to my partner. 'It's a pleasure to meet you. May I say he has done rather well for himself.'

Jenny looks at me as if unsure what to do before she shakes his hand out of politeness. Tellingly, Angus has not made an attempt to shake my hand, and I guess he isn't going to as he picks up his glass again.

'It's funny because Lachlan didn't have the best luck with members of the opposite sex when we were at school. Isn't that right, old pal?'

He puts a strong hand on my shoulder then, a move that could look friendly to a bystander, but to me, I know it carries the weight of something more sinister.

'How have you been, Angus?' I ask him, trying to take control of this exchange.

'Fortunately, I had better luck than he did,' Angus goes on, ignoring my question and turning to Jenny. 'I had a few girl-friends at school, which must have been hard for Lachlan, him being my best friend and all. I mean, nobody wants to see their best mate get all the girls, do they?'

'Maybe we should leave,' I suggest to Jenny, but she doesn't move, allowing Angus to keep going.

'It's not as if there were many girls in this village to choose from either,' he says, spinning his glass around and accidentally spilling a few drops on the table, not that he seems to care. 'That must have made it even harder for him. And then, to make it worse, I went and got with the best-looking girl in the village. You know who that was, don't you?'

Now he's looking back at me, but I don't reply.

'Paisley Hamilton,' Angus answers for Jenny's benefit. 'She was mine, and all the guys at school were jealous of me, including my best mate right here.'

'What's your point?' I ask him, growing tired of this talk.

'My point...' Angus says, leaning in, and the scent of alcohol is heavy on his breath. 'My point is that I was suspected of killing Paisley and my life has been a living hell ever since then. Yet, if you think about it, I was the one guy in this village, other than Paisley's father, of course, who wanted her alive more than anything. That's because she was infatuated with me. So, why would I kill her? Wouldn't it make more sense that it was some-body who wanted her for themselves but couldn't have her? Somebody who couldn't stand to see me have her instead? Somebody who got jealous? Somebody who took that jealousy out on me by instigating a fight? But if you ask me, I got off a lot more lightly than Paisley did, that's for sure.'

Such is the strength of the alcohol fumes coming from Angus, I could almost get high inhaling them. Yet I feel as sober as ever as I process his words before I glance at Jenny to see what she is making of them.

'What are you saying?' Jenny asks Angus, but that's where I have to draw the line.

'He's not saying anything because he's drunk, and he's angry and bitter that I made it out of this place and he didn't,' I say, answering for him. 'And while I doubt he killed Paisley, he doesn't have a clue who did kill her, just like everybody else. So he needs to move on with his life like I have done or he can carry on drinking himself to death in this village. Either way, we're done here.'

I stand up then and look at Jenny to follow me but as she goes to leave her seat, Angus shoots out a hand and grips her wrist before fixing her with a steely stare.

'How well do you know your husband?' Angus asks her as he keeps a tight hold of her. 'Do you know him as well as I do? You might be the kind of couple who are best friends now, but we were best friends before that and that means I know him just as well as you. At least I did back then, when it counts. That's when my girlfriend was murdered, and I had to deal with all the accusations. And what did Lachlan do? He finished the school and left, as if he couldn't wait to get away. I wonder why that was.'

He's said enough, and even he knows it because he lets go of Jenny, and she stands up. Angus sits back in his seat and finishes his whiskey with a strange, satisfied smirk on his face. It's as if he knows he has just thrown a wrench into my relationship, like I did to his when I took Paisley's life.

I only hope that, for me, it doesn't end like it did for him.

That would be with police questioning, serious suspicions and, worst-case scenario, with me drinking whiskey in a pub all by myself.

But what if that is the best-case scenario?

Things could certainly get much worse than that.

TWENTY-EIGHT

JENNY

'What is he trying to say?' I ask Lachlan as he leads me away from Angus and towards the back room of the pub where our children are playing pool. 'What is he getting at?'

'Just ignore him. He's drunk,' Lachlan replies as he carries on, until I say something that makes him stop.

'Does he think that *you* killed Paisley?' I ask, the question sounding almost ludicrous as soon as I've aired it, but it's the question on my mind, and the reason my heart is racing now.

Lachlan freezes, and when he looks back, I am waiting for him to tell me that this is the most ridiculous thing in the world and then give me a perfectly good explanation why Angus was the way he was with us just now.

But that doesn't happen.

'Hey, Lachlan! Do you want another drink?' one of the guys at the bar calls over and, annoyingly, it provides the temporary distraction that my husband needs to avoid answering me. But that's all it is, a temporary distraction, because I've been feeling more and more uneasy about everything to do with this place and the people within it as time has gone by and, most of all, if and how it is connected to why Lachlan left here in the first place.

'No, I'm leaving now,' Lachlan says, waving away the offer from his old friend. 'It was good to see you guys.'

He carries on his way then and enters the back room of the pub, so I follow him in and, when I do, I see William playing pool with a teenage local. It takes me a little longer to locate his sister. Then I see her, sitting in the corner beside a guy who looks around a year or two older than her.

They seem to be sharing a joke.

They also seem to be sharing an alcoholic drink.

'Come on, time to go,' Lachlan says as he gestures to William before spotting what is in Bonnie's hand just like I did. 'Put that down. You're underage.'

Bonnie looks as frustrated and embarrassed as any seventeen-year-old would be when told to stop doing something in front of her peers. It's uncool, but it's not out of order because Lachlan is right. Our daughter shouldn't be drinking. Now she has stopped, though she isn't happy about it. William isn't happy about the interruption either, as his game of pool is unfinished and that's not something that has age-limit laws, but Lachlan doesn't care.

'We're going. Come on,' he repeats, and clearly aware that their father could make even more of a scene that would only embarrass them both further, Bonnie and William do as they are told and follow us out.

'Text me,' the guy Bonnie was just chatting to shouts after her, but I don't have the chance to ask her who he was or why she has apparently already given him her phone number because we're outside in the fresh air and neither of our kids is happy.

The steps leading up to our room are just a few feet away, but Bonnie and William are frustrated, and as I quickly learn, a little tipsy.

'What did you do that for?' Bonnie cries.

'Yeah, we were having fun,' William says, on his sister's side for once.

'You shouldn't be drinking,' Lachlan says. 'Neither of you.'

'I'm nearly eighteen,' Bonnie moans. 'I'm old enough to make my own decisions now.'

'No, you're not,' Lachlan goes on, heading for the stairs. 'That boy is only interested in you for one reason. He wants to get you drunk and then he wants to take you some place quiet and—'

'Lachlan!' I cry, cutting him off.

He stops at the foot of the stairs and seems surprised at the volume of my voice, but it came from a place of genuine frustration. He's right in what he is saying, I guess, but he's going about it the wrong way. This is not the best way to get Bonnie or William to do what he wants. It's also not the best way to get me to do what he wants either and that's the crux of the problem.

Ever since we got here, Lachlan has tried to control us, manipulate and manoeuvre us around, as if he doesn't trust us to figure things out for ourselves. All he keeps saying is that this place is not a good place and the sooner we leave, the better. But I'm starting to think he is protesting too much. He's been uncomfortable in every conversation he's had here, and the time has come for him to explain to me and the kids why that is. If not, he will have to find some other poor people to take his frustration out on.

'What is going on with you?' I ask him, not caring that Bonnie and William will hear this. 'What's happened to my husband? What's happened to their father? I don't recognise the man standing in front of me anymore. What has made you like this?'

Lachlan takes his time coming up with an answer but all three of us are happy to wait for it.

'Are you on my side or not?' he eventually asks.

'What?'

'I said, are you on my side, the side of your husband, or are you not?'

'I don't understand what you mean by that,' I reply, genuinely confused.

'I mean, I warned you about this place,' Lachlan goes on. 'How it's full of small-minded people with grand delusions, people who have nothing to do all day but dream up fantastical theories about what happened to the one person who was murdered here. I tried to shield you from this place and these people because they are losers who have nothing going for them. They are not me and I am not them. And you, Bonnie, drinking with that guy. He's a loser like the rest of them. Can't you see it? I want better for you. I want better for us all. That's why I left here and started a family elsewhere, away from this hellhole of a place where a poor girl got killed once. Although the truth is, it was an awful place before that, and it always will be. So, are you on my side, or are you on theirs?'

That's quite the speech from my husband, certainly an impassioned one, and it deserves a good response.

'I'm on your side, of course I am,' I say, but there's a caveat. 'But I have questions. The same questions everyone here has. Who killed Paisley and why? In the pub just then, Angus seemed to suggest he thought you had something to do with it.'

'Angus thinks Dad killed Paisley?' Bonnie cries, forgetting about the embarrassment of the pub and latching on to this new and dramatic thread.

'Yes, he does,' I say. 'That doesn't mean I think your father did it, but I want to know why people suspect him. An innocent person can experience a lot of things in life, but it's very rare for them to be seen as a murder suspect without good reason. So start talking, Lachlan. Tell me what you've failed to tell me so far. Tell me everything you know about Paisley's death.'

'You can tell me too while I'm here,' a voice behind me says, and I turn around to see Paisley's father standing behind us.

I'm not sure if he has come out of the pub or was on his way inside, but he's overheard us and now he's joined this tricky debate.

'There's nothing to tell,' Lachlan says with a shake of the head. 'Except...'

'Except what?' Mr Hamilton asks, and I hold my breath because I'm not sure what is coming next.

'Except that your daughter, the famous and tragic Paisley Hamilton, was not the sweet and innocent girl everyone seems to think she was,' Lachlan says, which is a very serious and strange thing to say to her father.

'What do you mean by that?' comes the next obvious question.

'I'm just saying, she was a popular girl and an attractive one and Angus wasn't the only guy she was with,' Lachlan goes on, seemingly warming to his theme. 'She was never with me, but she was with others, guys you probably don't even know about and guys I don't even know the name of because sometimes people pass through from the cities, you know that. So, I'm telling you that one of those guys must have killed her, and considering how she was in the woods at night, she had obviously gone there with that person to do something she probably shouldn't. So she's not Miss Perfect, which is why it's unfair for people here to speculate on others and try and point out their flaws too.'

Lachlan should probably leave it there given who he is talking to, but he doesn't, and I wince as he says his final line.

'The truth is, if your daughter was in the woods late at night then she was up to no good. So she has to take some blame for what happened to her.'

I glance at Mr Hamilton to see what he has made of that and I'm expecting him to erupt. After absorbing it, he lets out a deep sigh and turns towards the pub door. As he goes, I realise this is a man who has lost the energy to argue after all he has been through in life. Just before he enters the pub, he looks back at my husband and says something that would send a chill down the spine of any parent.

'I don't blame the killer for what happened to my daughter,' he says forlornly. 'And I certainly don't blame her like you say I should. The truth is, I blame myself. I let my guard down. I allowed her to get close to danger without realising it and then it was too late. Because that's the thing about life. We hear about terrible things on the news, but they always seem so far away, like they'll never happen to us. But often, most likely, the danger in our lives is closer than we think. Sometimes, it's staring us right in the face.'

With that, Mr Hamilton goes into the pub, leaving the four of us outside with his words still hanging in the air.

I look at my daughter, then my son, before finally, my eyes land on my husband.

As they do, I think about the last sentence the grieving father of the murdered woman just said and, for some reason, it doesn't seem like it was only a generic warning.

It feels more like it was a specific warning for me.

TWENTY-NINE

LACHLAN

The last thing anybody needs after a terrible night's sleep is an argument. But it seems that's what I'm going to get because despite hoping for a simple agreement, my wife is against the idea I have just proposed.

'The car should be fixed now, so let's all get in it and go home,' I had said once everyone was awake. 'We can drop William off at the festival and the rest of us can go back to our house. This holiday has been a bit of a disaster, so we might as well write it off and try again some other time.'

I felt like that was a fair assessment of how things had gone since we came to Scotland, and rather than prolong our misery and allow more problems to occur, I figure it's best we quit while we're behind and return to home comforts. Of course, if I was to return home with all my family in tow, it would mean I wouldn't have the opportunity to visit Francesca, but I'll have to put my plans for her on hold for a while. These last few days have been an unexpected disruption, and I'd rather get Jenny out of here than leave her in this village any longer where she might be susceptible to suspicions and theories.

If it's not already too late.

As someone who hides a dark secret, I can sense when another person is doing the same. Considering my wife has been with me since yesterday, I believe she is withholding something from me, or at least trying to. Something important. Something like her thinking there might be some truth to what Angus said in the pub.

I think the best thing for me to do is to get Jenny home and then assess things from there. I'm praying she hasn't had her head filled with doubts about me and the man I am.

If she has, that could be a very big problem.

For her.

'No, Bonnie and I are staying here as planned,' Jenny says, declining the invitation for me to drive us all back home. 'You take William to the festival if the car is fixed then come back and we can stay here and go and visit Edinburgh before we go home tomorrow.'

That's not what I wanted to hear, and I don't like the way she has just volunteered to stay here. It makes me think she is trying to buy more time in this village. To do what? It's certainly not to go shopping or sightseeing, because there's nothing like that to do here. The only thing she can do is talk to the locals, so that must be what she wants. But that's the last thing I want, her listening to more salacious gossip, and as such, I'm willing to rearrange what I was already planning.

'No, it's too much driving back and forth for me,' I say, shaking my head. 'I know it was my idea originally, but it's silly for me and William to go all the way back and then return for you guys, all for the sake of an extra day here. I'm tired. I don't think I can do it.'

Will that work? Feigning exhaustion? Trying for sympathy because it would involve many miles of motorway for me? It doesn't matter, as it doesn't work.

'Have a great time at the festival,' Jenny says to William as he excitedly gets ready. She looks to our daughter. 'Bonnie, how about we buy a few things from the shop and go for a picnic in the woods?'

'Sure,' Bonnie replies far too quickly, no doubt because she's morbidly desperate to find the spot where Paisley died.

'Seriously, you want a picnic in the place where a woman was killed?' I ask, shaking my head at my wife.

'No, the woods are big, we can find another spot,' she says casually, which I guess is true. The woods are big. I should know. It's their size that allowed me to go unseen on the night I took a life. I still hate the idea of Jenny and Bonnie staying here, especially with people like Angus around. But if they are determined, maybe I'll have to stay, so I turn to my son.

'William, I'm really sorry about this, but I'm not going to be able to drive you back,' I tell him as his face falls.

'What?' he cries.

'It's too far and it's silly of us to split up, so if your mum and sister are staying here, so are we.'

'That's not fair. You promised him,' Jenny says. 'He's going to that festival, and you are taking him. Now go to the garage and get the car and we'll see you when you're back.'

Jenny really wants me out of here, which only makes me even more paranoid.

'Can you kids give us a minute?' I ask, and Bonnie and William each let out a sigh before trudging out of the room, no doubt bored by now of all their parents' disagreements.

'Are we okay?' I ask my wife once we're alone.

'Why wouldn't we be?'

'You're being weird with me.'

'Am I?'

'Yes, you know you are. So what's it all about?'

'Not everything's a big conspiracy,' Jenny says then, patting me on the arm with a slightly condescending smile. 'Stop worrying so much. Go and spend some quality time with William. You're doing him a big favour and I'm sure he's very grateful. But he won't be if you're late to that festival, so best be on your way.'

I stare into my wife's eyes, the same eyes I looked into as we stood at the altar in front of all our loved ones, but something is different to what I saw on our wedding day. Back then, I saw nothing but love, which made sense because I had worked hard to make her think that I was perfect. But now? I see doubt, which unfortunately also makes sense because since being back here, plenty of doubt has been cast on me and my behaviour.

I realise I need to keep calm and not lose my cool, so I act as if everything is okay and give Jenny a kiss before leaving, finding William on the stairs outside and, after we say goodbye to Bonnie, the pair of us head for the garage.

When we get there, we find the mechanic in a good mood and that's because he has finished work on our car as promised and is ready to accept full payment. I use his electronic card machine to transfer him the funds while William gets in the passenger seat, eager to get on the road sooner rather than later. It's still early and traffic should be light for most of the way, but he doesn't want to take any chances, so once I'm done with the mechanic, I get in behind the wheel and start the engine.

I should be thrilled about the fact that I'm driving out of this village now, having spent so long wanting to be away from it. But that's not the case. I'm worried Jenny is on to me and my hidden past.

I try telling myself that's not the reality though. If she thought I had killed Paisley, if she was seriously entertaining that idea, then she surely wouldn't let me just drive off with our son. She'd want to make sure her children were safe, which means she still thinks he is safe with me. That's good, but it doesn't mean she isn't going to do some digging around while I'm gone to try and uncover some more opinions on the murder.

There's no evidence, I think to myself as William sits in the passenger seat beside me, totally oblivious to the inner turmoil of his father as he listens to music and looks forward to the festival. People can speculate all they like, even Jenny, if she wants to. But nobody can prove a thing. I've got away with this for twenty-five years and I'll get away with it for another twenty-five.

But just in case I'm wrong and Jenny does somehow figure it out, I will have no choice but to deal with her. She might be my wife but she's not immune to the threat I pose. Like any other woman who crosses me, I will act if I need to. Sure, I'd feel bad for Bonnie and William if anything happened to their mother, but if it comes down to me or her, there can only be one winner.

The further I drive away from the village, it's as if I feel my confidence returning. That place really does sap the energy out of me, but the more miles I put between myself and it, the more I am reminded that I am good at what I do. Not just good. *Great.*

I'm so great that I stop worrying about my wife and start thinking about another woman I want to deal with.

Maybe I will go and see Francesca while William is at the festival. Maybe it's what I need to remind myself who is the boss.

It's never been Jenny.

I've always done a brilliant job of making her think it is.

THIRTY

JENNY

As we enter the woods, it's impossible not to be struck by the natural beauty of the area. The pine trees are tall and majestic, flowers are in full bloom, the local birdlife is in full song and Bonnie and I even catch sight of a deer prancing through the undergrowth before disappearing into the dense foliage.

Unfortunately, it's impossible not to be struck by something else too.

The thought that it was in here where Paisley Hamilton took her last breath.

I don't know how to find the exact location of her death as we move deeper into the woods while seeking out a suitable picnic spot, nor do I intend to try and figure it out. In fact, I'm just about thinking it wasn't the best idea to come here when Bonnie suddenly points out a place she thinks will work.

'Over there,' she says, pointing into the distance and, when I look, I see a natural break in the trees beside what appears to be a stream cutting through this luscious, green place.

As I follow my daughter, I hear the rippling and running of the water. Bonnie is right. This is a perfect place for a picnic. It's so beautiful, in fact, that it causes me to temporarily forget about the awful thing that happened somewhere around here and just enjoy being with my daughter in nature.

As I set out the rug I borrowed from the owner of the pub, and Bonnie starts unpacking the items we picked up in the shop, I try to focus on the present. This is a great chance for some quality time with Bonnie before she goes to university and that's exactly what the whole point of this trip to Scotland was. I've been so swept up in the past since getting here, as everyone else in this village seems to be, but there's nothing like the wonder of the Scottish wilderness to clear the mind.

'What shall we have first?' I ask as Bonnie and I work together to open up packets of foods that range in their variety from sausage rolls and breadsticks to olives and crisps.

'Let's just nibble on it all,' Bonnie replies, which is the right answer because what is a picnic if not picking at everything on offer all at once?

As we tuck into our food and enjoy sips from our own bottles of cold diet cola, I look around at various beautiful things, from the way the sunlight breaks through the trees and hits the surface of the stream to the colourful flowers and the way they add some vivid individuality to this picturesque scene. But most of all, I look at my daughter's face and how she has grown from a cheeky child into an almost full-fledged woman.

'I'm proud of you,' I say, smiling, as I mean it.

'Huh?' Bonnie replies, her mouth full of food and even more of it in her hand ready to be shovelled in.

I laugh before finishing a bite of my own nibbles and speaking again.

'I just want you to know that I'm very proud of the person you have grown up to be. And I know you're going to go on and do many amazing things, at university and beyond.'

'Mum, there's no need to be soppy. It's just a picnic,' Bonnie says, rolling her eyes.

'No, I mean it. You really make me proud. I just wanted you to know.'

'Thanks,' Bonnie says, pausing her eating for a second to show genuine gratitude. 'Do you think Dad feels the same way?'

'Yes, of course. Why do you say that?'

'I don't know. He always seems so frustrated with me.'

'Does he?'

'You know he does. He has a go at me about everything. College work. What time I get in from seeing friends. He embarrassed me in front of everyone in the pub last night.'

'You shouldn't have been drinking alcohol with that guy,' I remind her, giving Lachlan a pass for reprimanding her for that.

'Okay, fine. But what about the documentary? Why did he shout at me over that? Even you have to admit that it is a weird thing to get angry at me about.'

Bonnie is right. It felt weird at the time, but I put it down to Lachlan just being tetchy about the place of his birth. But now we've been back here and I've seen how he has behaved, it's not as if he's any more relaxed about it. Even with so many school friends warmly welcoming him and offering to buy him drinks, he has remained steadfast in his hatred of this place, which is strange.

'What's going on with Dad?' Bonnie asks me as she picks up a breadstick. 'He's been even weirder than usual since we got here. It's like he's hiding something from us.'

The beauty of the moment and this scenic setting is quickly receding from my mind, and I'm back to thinking about Angus and how he asked me how well I knew my husband.

'Hello? Earth to Mum?' Bonnie says, and I snap out of my trance, unaware that I'd been in it long enough to make my daughter realise I wasn't listening to her.

'Sorry,' I say, shaking my head and picking up my drink.

'What's wrong? It's Dad, isn't it? Are you okay?'

'Yeah, we're fine. Why wouldn't we be?'

'You've been arguing. He's been weird. He crashed our car. You didn't want to go with him today. Why are you falling out with each other?'

How do I answer that? How do I tell my daughter that the reason my relationship with her father is struggling is because I'm starting to worry that he knows more about Paisley's death than he is letting on.

'It's quite chilly here,' I say, making up a reason to change the subject. 'And a little creepy. Maybe we should head back into the village.'

'We just got here,' Bonnie says, but I've made up my mind and I start packing the leftover food away.

Bonnie lets out a sigh as she gives up, and not wanting to be out here alone, she helps me finish the tidying up before we get to our feet and, once the rug is folded up and under my arm, we start walking back the way we came. Although with my thoughts so clouded, and Bonnie muttering away about how this trip has been a waste of time, the pair of us fail to realise that we are going the wrong way. That's until we come to another clearing, one with no stream in it this time, and while I have never been here before, it seems strangely familiar for some reason. Then Bonnie figures out why.

'This is where her body was found,' she says as we look around the clearing, before my daughter points to a large fallen tree that I realise was shown in the documentary.

The tree is surrounded by bouquets of flowers, most of them fresh, and I wonder if they have been left by those who knew Paisley intimately before she died or people who have watched the recent documentary and felt compelled to leave their own mark here.

I feel a chill run through my body before I look up and see that the sunlight is almost totally blocked by the canopy of the trees in this part of the woods, which could explain the sudden drop in temperature. Or maybe we are in the presence of death, albeit twenty-five years on.

But then I hear a sound, a twig snapping behind me, and as I spin around, the hair on the back of my neck stands on end and makes me think that the reason I felt so cold a moment ago is because there is somebody else out here with us.

Is there?

Is somebody watching us?

If so, who are they?

'We need to go,' I say to Bonnie, and she must be feeling the same fear, as she doesn't argue, so the pair of us pick a direction and walk quickly away from the site of the bloody crime.

But while we are successful in putting distance between us and the place where Paisley passed, we are not successful in shaking the feeling that a third person was just with us back there.

I don't know who they might have been or what they were doing. Like everything here, it's a mystery. As we eventually find our way out of the woods and re-enter the village, I make a vow to myself.

I'm done with the mystery of this place.

It's time I got some answers.

It's time to find out what is really going on with my husband.

THIRTY-ONE

LACHLAN

The sight of hordes of teenagers walking in the same direction is a strong sign that we're in the right place for the festival, and as William unbuckles his seatbelt, I look around and ask the obvious question.

'How are you going to find your friends?'

'We're meeting over there,' my son says before checking his hair in the sun-visor mirror, an indicator that he cares enough about who he will be seeing shortly to make sure he is looking his best.

It's obvious that his desperation to not miss this event is linked to that girl he has a crush on at his school, so before he departs, I feel it apt to try and pass on a few words of wisdom.

'Have a good day. And remember, if there's someone you like, tell them. You might be pleasantly surprised.'

'Whatever,' William replies casually, not interested in any advice I have, despite the fact that he would do very well to listen to a person who has done a lot more in life than he has.

'Okay, so I'll pick you back up from this spot here, got it?' I say, making sure he can find me easily enough when this afternoon festival ends in a few hours' time.

'Yep. See you later,' William says, getting out of the car and following the crowds, and very quickly, I lose sight of my son in the throngs of teens.

I hope he has a good day, and I hope it was worth him making me drive all the way back here. But that remains to be seen, and I guess I'll get a good idea of that when I collect him later and get a sense of the kind of mood he is in. If there's a big, dopey grin on his face then I will presume it went well and he maybe even got a kiss from his crush. If he looks gloomy, I guess I'll have to deal with teen angst during the return trip to Scotland.

While I can't control the kind of day my son has, I can control mine, and as I drive away from the festival, my thoughts turn to Francesca. Like my son, I am interested in a woman. Unlike him, I already know that I stand little chance of ever being with her. She's made that clear with how uninterested she has been in me in the office. It's also obvious who she likes by how engaged she has been with the other male in the office who has shown her an interest.

There's no point denying it. She doesn't want to be with me.

That's okay, it's her right.

But it's also my right to do something about it.

Despite my concerns about Jenny and what she might be doing in Carnfield, I find myself driving in the direction of Francesca's house. That's a pretty strong indicator that despite recent stresses, I am still willing to kill again and make her my third victim. I remind myself that nobody other than my family knows I am here, so if I can do this efficiently and return to Scotland with William as if everything is normal, I can get away with this. Sure, there will be a news report when Francesca's body is found, and it will be one that Jenny sees, but hopefully she won't learn that Francesca works at the same place as me and ever make a connection between us there. And hopefully, nobody else will make a connection between us either and I'll never be a suspect.

Just like with Teri, I can get away with it. And just like with Paisley, I could be looking back on this day in twenty-five years' time and chuckling to myself about how easy it all ended up being.

As I park a couple of streets away from Francesca's place, I look around at the other houses and try to ascertain if any of the homeowners around here might pose a problem for me. I don't want a nosey neighbour watching me or getting involved in my business, and even though I have a baseball cap on, I'd still prefer to be unnoticed. But I can't see anybody out here. The street is quiet, that midday suburban lull that sometimes drives me mad is serving me well now, and I tell myself that even if somebody does look through a window and sees me walking along their street, why would they think anything of it? I'd just be a pedestrian like any other.

I get out of my car and start walking to the next street, each step taking me closer to taking a life, and when I turn the corner and see the house I am here to visit, I feel that familiar thrill I have felt before.

Paisley. Teri. Now Francesca.

They say everything comes in threes.

I guess that also applies to murder.

I'm only about ten feet away from Francesca's house when I see her front door open, causing me to duck down behind a neighbour's wall to ensure I'm not seen. As I peer back over, I see my target standing on her doorstep in her dressing gown.

But she is not alone.

She's saying goodbye to somebody and when I see who it is, I feel the same burning sense of envy and anger I felt when I was watching Paisley with Angus. It's Rich, my younger and better-looking colleague, and he has clearly just spent the night with Francesca. The pair of them look happy, basking in the warm afterglow of a night together, and as he walks away with a spring in his step, I wish I could wipe that smug look off his face. But he's not the one I want. Not really. It's her. She's the one who rejected me. So I remain in my hiding place until he has got in his car and left. Then, as Francesca closes her door, I briskly walk towards it, emboldened by my previous reconnaissance trip here where I checked and failed to see any doorbell cameras or other forms of surveillance around the property.

There's no going back now.

As I knock on the door, I think about how the man who just left might end up being viewed as the prime suspect when Francesca's murder is investigated, especially if anyone else knew he was here. It sure would help me if his car was seen parked outside here all night before she was killed. I don't care if the wrong man gets accused of a crime. I only care about getting away with the crime myself, and as the door opens, I take a deep breath. Here we go again.

'Back for more already?' Francesca laughs as I see her smiling, though it's a smile that quickly fades when she realises I am not Rich, the man who has just been in her house. I am the man she desperately needs to keep out of her house. But now the door is open, and as I have caught her by surprise, it's easy for me to push my way in and overpower her.

As she screams and tries to fight me off, I drag her towards her kitchen and my aim is to find a sharp knife to use as the murder weapon. I know I've used a knife before, but it's quick and efficient, and time is of the essence here.

As Francesca starts making too much noise, I hit her and she falls down, instantly giving me a flashback to the time both Paisley and Teri did the same thing. The familiar and intoxicating feeling of pure power washes over me as I look at my victim lying by my feet as I pick up a knife and prepare to use it. Before I can, I hear a knock at the front door.

It causes me to stop, and even Francesca stops too, no longer crying or screaming, but momentarily wondering if she is going to be saved after all. Then we hear a voice.

'Hey! Sorry, it's me again. I think I left my phone behind.'

It's Rich, and I realise he isn't going to leave until he has his phone back, which is problematic for me because he is now blocking my escape route. But I figure I could slip out of the back door, so I turn to Francesca and raise my knife, still committed to carrying out this crime

But she is no longer where I last saw her.

She is back to her feet now and running towards the door. In a truly horrifying second, I realise I'm not going to be able to catch up to her before she opens it.

I'm about to be caught. This is it. This must be how it ends for me.

I'm not ready to face justice so I turn and run the other way, pulling the back door open and taking off and even though I hear shouting behind me, I keep sprinting until I have made it back to my parked car. Then I get in and start the engine, sweating profusely and trying not to have a panic attack before I can get away from here and figure out my next move.

I shouldn't have come here. It was a risk too far. But I took it, and I have paid the price.

The two careful crimes I not only committed in the past but got away with are going to be undone by this third, more reckless crime I attempted.

I should have quit while I was ahead. I could have got away with it all. But now the truth about me is going to come out and I'm not sure what I'm afraid of the most.

The police?

The victims' families?

Or my wife?

THIRTY-TWO

JENNY

I check the time and wonder why Bonnie isn't here yet. After we abandoned our picnic in the woods and came back into the village, I planned for the pair of us to hang out together in the room while we waited for Lachlan and William to return. But just before we got back here, Bonnie said she wanted to get some chocolate from the shop and would meet me in the room afterwards. I offered to go with her, but she said she would only be a couple of minutes, so I left her and returned to the room, unburdening myself of the blanket and the food items that had survived the picnic. But it's been half an hour now and there's still no sign of her.

So where is she?

I'm probably being paranoid, but still shaken from the sense of being watched in the woods, I decide to go out and look for my daughter. Heading out onto the street, I make my way to the shop because that's where she said she was going. I can't see why she could have got held up there for long just to buy as simple an item as a bar of chocolate, but she must have done. Maybe one of the locals got talking to her. I wonder if Gerard initiated a conversation with her. That man is so chatty that

Bonnie could easily have found herself stuck talking to him for longer than she wanted to.

As I enter the shop, I'm expecting to find her bored and in need of rescuing as Gerard regales her with some tale of her father when he was younger. But while I see him in his uniform, diligently stacking a shelf, I don't see her.

'Hey, back again? We're not used to such regular custom in here,' Gerard jokes when he sees me. 'What do you need this time?'

'Erm, just my daughter, actually,' I say, looking around. 'Have you seen her? She was coming in here to get some chocolate about half an hour ago.'

'Nope, you're the first customer I've seen in the last half an hour,' Gerard says. 'But don't worry, that's very normal. We're usually quiet this time of day.'

While it might be normal for him, it's not normal for me to have lost my daughter.

'Are you sure you haven't seen her? She said she was coming in here.'

'I'm absolutely certain. I see everyone who comes in and she definitely hasn't.'

I realise then that Bonnie must have lied to me about coming here, which worries me. But then a larger worry emerges. What if she was telling the truth but never made it here because somebody intervened?

What if she is in danger now?

I quickly leave the shop, ignoring Gerard's calls asking if I'm okay, and run out onto the street where I look around in all directions for any sign of my daughter. I can't see her and while this place is not the biggest, that doesn't matter because as any parent who has lost their child would know, it's frightening whatever the environment.

'She's okay. She's seventeen,' I tell myself, needing the reminder that she is not a young, helpless baby but a woman who could potentially fight off any danger if needed. But could she?

Or what if she was overpowered?

Like Paisley was?

I wish Lachlan was here. Despite our recent issues, he would surely know what to do. He'd tell me that there must be a simple explanation for this and that I needed to stay calm, and while that would be easier said than done, there would be some comfort to be found in his lack of panic. But he is not here, I am all by myself, and I have no idea who might be with Bonnie, so my panic is increasing by the second.

I start running through the village while looking left and right and when I see an elderly woman walking towards me with a shopping bag, I cry out to her.

'Have you seen my daughter? She's seventeen! Dark hair! About this tall!' I say, using my hand to give a rough gauge of her height.

'No, I'm sorry,' the woman replies, looking startled, probably as she didn't expect to encounter a desperate woman on her way to the shop.

I run past her and keep searching, but still no luck, until I hear a voice calling out to me.

'What's the matter? You look like you've lost something.'

I spin around to see Angus sitting on a bench with a plastic bag beside him and an open can of beer in his hand. It looks like he is comfortable there with his drink, which I doubt is his first of the day, and he certainly looks amused as he watches me struggling to contain my emotions.

'Have you seen my daughter?' I ask him, figuring that while he may be drunk, he could still be useful.

'Beautiful Bonnie? No, I haven't,' Angus replies with a shrug. 'Care to join me for a drink? I have plenty here.'

Angus pats his plastic bag then and specifically, the box of beers he has inside.

Why did he refer to her as beautiful Bonnie? Just making a passing comment on how pretty she is, like any kind person might do when discussing somebody's daughter, because that's nicer than saying they are ugly. Or is there something more sinister to it?

Has he been attracted to her and, in his drunken state, done something terrible?

'Where is she? What have you done?' I cry as I run towards the bench, blindly deciding that this man is involved in her disappearance somehow. Maybe it's the way he is so calmly sitting there while I am losing control that is driving me towards him. Or maybe it's the fact that he was suspected of the murder of a woman of similar age to my daughter in the past, so he is as good a suspect as any. Either way, he is about to experience my wrath unless he starts talking.

'Woah, there. Calm down. I've got nothing to hide,' Angus says, raising his hands, one of which still has a beer in it. 'Like I told you in the pub yesterday, I didn't hurt Paisley, so there's no need to be afraid of me.'

'Prove it!' I cry, picking up his plastic bag full of beer cans and intimating that I'm prepared to throw them on the floor and potentially spill all the liquid inside them unless he can do what I just asked.

'What? How do I do that?' he says, sitting forward on the bench and clearly anxious for the safety of his beers.

'You must have seen her if you've been sitting here,' I tell him. 'This is such a small place, you had to have seen her, so you'll know which way she went. So prove to me that you aren't the terrible person that everybody thinks you are and help me! Help my daughter!'

Angus takes that on board and it's as if all he has ever wanted is the chance to show that he is not the guy who got away with murder.

'I saw her,' he admits then. 'She was with some guy. I think he was in the pub last night.'

I quickly realise who he must mean. It'll be the guy she was drinking with before Lachlan dragged her out of there. I also remember that the guy called after Bonnie as she was leaving, telling her to send him a text message. I guess she must have done that and that's how the pair of them set up their secret meeting. The trip to the shop to get chocolate was just a ruse to lose me.

'Where are they now? Which way did they go?' I ask, looking all around again but still not seeing them.

'They're just young kids,' Angus says with a wistful look. 'Let them have their fun and she'll soon be back.'

'Which way?' I repeat, my voice threatening to be loud enough to rattle the foundations of this sleepy village.

'That way,' Angus says, eventually pointing me in a direction.

It's the direction of the woods – the woods where Paisley died – and the woods where it felt like somebody was watching me earlier.

I guess I'm going back in there again.

THIRTY-THREE

LACHLAN

For a man who has committed murder and attempted murder, breaking a few traffic laws is child's play, which is why I am not concerning myself with how fast I am driving as I race towards the festival to get my son. My plan is to find William and then head north to Scotland as soon as possible, before the police can catch up with me.

Before I lose my family.

Before I lose it all.

Francesca must have already called the police by now after my ill-fated attempt on her life was interrupted, and thanks to me not wearing a disguise, she will have given them my name. I'm regretting not wearing a balaclava now, but I didn't think this would be a problem. Francesca should have been dead by now. Things have never gone awry for me like they have here.

Police officers in the area will presumably be out looking for anybody fleeing the scene. I was quick when I got away so I should be ahead of them all, at least for a short while. But my window of opportunity will diminish rapidly the longer I linger here, which is why it is imperative that I locate my son and get him in this car with me before I go to rejoin my wife and daughter.

As of yet, I don't know what I will do when I am with them. I'll make a plan when I'm on the motorway. For now, all that matters is that I get the chance to be with them one last time before everything totally unravels and they discover the man I really am.

As I return to the same spot where William exited my car earlier today, the scene looks a lot different than it did back then. There are no large crowds of teenagers now and that's because they are all on the other side of the perimeter fences, at the festival, dancing to the music and having the kind of fun that I'll never have again. The only people I can see out here with me are the security staff who stand by the gates that lead beyond the fences, and they are the people I'm going to have to get past if I am to get inside and find William as quickly as possible.

I get out of my car and run towards them and when they see me coming, the security staff frown, as I don't look like the typical customer for a festival aimed at teens. One of them even puts their hand up as if I need reminding that this event is not for me, but I can't let that stop me from accomplishing my goal.

'Hi, guys,' I say breathlessly as I stop in front of them. 'My son's inside and I really need to find him. There's a family emergency. I've tried calling him, but he's not answering. I guess there's no signal in there. Please, can you let me in so I can get to him?'

I'm hoping that's a good enough excuse to pass security, but is it?

'Family emergency?' one of the security staff says, chewing gum and looking as bored as anybody might be guarding an event for youngsters. 'What kind of emergency?'

'It's his mother. She's just been admitted to hospital and she's going to have to have an operation, but she really wants to see him before they sedate her because there are risks and she might not wake up and—'

'Woah, calm down there,' another security guard says, and this one looks a lot more sympathetic to my plight, albeit a totally fictional plight.

He looks to his colleague and confers quietly with him for a second before they give me their answer.

'Okay, come with me,' the friendlier security man says, and he opens the gate and steps inside, leaving it open for me to walk in after him.

It's a relief to be in, but my task is by no means over. As I look around at the hundreds of people in here, I have no idea how I am supposed to find William quickly. Add to that, many of them are moving around, walking, or dancing to the loud music, and it's a very chaotic, confusing scene.

Not what I need after what has already happened today.

'So, what does he look like?' the security guard asks me as he presumably figures this is going to take a while to sort out. I don't have much time and I feel like being with him will only hinder my progress rather than help it, so I need to ditch him fast.

'I think that's him. Over there!' I cry, pointing to his left, but while he looks that way, I quickly dart off in the other direction and seamlessly slip into the crowd.

Now I'm alone, I begin my search properly, scanning the sea of faces as I move among them, searching for my boy, desperate to find him before the police can find me.

There is so much I still wanted to teach him, life lessons, the kind only a father can give, but is any of that possible now or is our relationship over?

All I know is that I can't give up. I can't leave here without him and run away on my own. For all I have done wrong, I love my children, and I need time with them before whatever happens next.

'William!' I call out in the vain hope that he might luckily be nearby and hear me, but even if he is, the deafening music drowns out my cries.

I keep moving, always looking, hoping to get fortunate and bump into him. But no luck so far.

It takes me about ten minutes to make it through the crowd and now I'm on the other side of this festival to where I entered it, and I'm just about to begin my second sweep when I catch a glimpse of him. I see William over by the fence, walking by himself, a plastic cup in one hand, and he is moving with purpose. I look ahead of where he is going and see several mobile toilets, the kind that are so common at outdoor public events like this, so I figure that is where he is going.

I move in that direction, aiming to intercept him, and while I consider calling out again, I know the music will only do the same thing as last time and render my voice obsolete, so I leave it.

I'm getting close to William now but just before I can reach him, I see him walk down the side of the toilets, which surprises me as I thought he was going to use one of them. He's gone behind them and when I follow him around the back, I see why. While I'm following him, he has been following somebody else.

It's her, the girl I saw him watching outside school.

His crush.

And she is with somebody else.

I pause when William does and while he is a few yards in front of me, he has no idea I'm behind him. He's too busy watching the two teens in front of him. They are kissing, using the privacy in this quieter part of the festival to have an intimate moment rather than be out there among the crowd.

I guess my son did not get the girl.

Just like I didn't get Paisley, or Teri, or Francesca.

But he is watching somebody else get his girl, just like I have done before, and I realise that history might be repeating itself here.

That's when I wonder if my son has inherited the same tendencies I possessed.

If he can't have the girl, *nobody can.*

When I see him throw down his plastic cup and clench his fists before taking a step towards the oblivious couple, I can sense his anger and frustration, and it appears he is about to take it out on them. But before he can do that, I run towards him and put a hand on his shoulder, stopping him.

As he spins around, his eyes go wide when he realises I am here.

'Dad, what are you doing?' he asks me, but I ignore that.

'What are you doing?' I ask him in return.

'Nothing,' he tries, and behind him, the young couple are still kissing, with no idea we are here.

'It's not worth it,' I tell him then. 'Whatever it was you were about to do, don't do it. They are not worth it. Just leave them alone.'

'I don't know what you're talking about,' William tries lamely, but his emotions quickly get the better of him because it's impossible to conceal a broken heart and a damaged ego – and he soon admits it.

'I liked her,' he says sadly.

'I know,' I reply, pulling him in for a hug, and as I grip him, this feels like more than just a simple expression of my support for him.

This feels like it might be the last time I ever get to do this.

'I hate her,' he says then, his head still on my shoulder. 'And I hate him.'

I realise he really does feel how I always feel when someone I like chooses somebody else over me, but importantly, he has not been able to act on it like I have done in the past and maybe, with a bit of luck, he never will.

'Listen to me,' I say as I put my hands on his shoulders and get him to look at me so I know he is listening. 'I know it hurts, but it's not her fault. She's entitled to be with whoever she wants to be and if that's not you, it's hard but it's okay. There will be somebody else out there who does want to be with you, and you've got to get over this disappointment and keep looking. Do you understand?'

I'm trying to teach my son something I have always known myself yet failed to grasp and it's why my life has been punctuated with violence against those who rejected me.

William has tears in his eyes, but he seems to appreciate the lesson I am trying to teach him as he nods, and I'm grateful for that because this is really important. This is just one of the reasons I needed to find him, like I need to find Bonnie and Jenny before the police catch me. I need to ensure they don't ever make the same mistakes I did. They have to be better than me.

History cannot repeat itself.

I'm the bad apple in the family.

I need to make sure I haven't poisoned the whole basket before I pay the price for it.

THIRTY-FOUR

JENNY

The woods that surround this village harbour secrets, the biggest one of which is who killed Paisley Hamilton. Right now, the only thing I want to know is where is my daughter.

Angus told me he saw her going in here with the guy she was with in the pub last night, but so far, despite looking, I haven't been able to locate either of them.

Are they here? Was Angus telling me the truth? Or did he deliberately mislead me because he's hiding something and he really is a person who is not to be trusted?

I'm trying to stay calm but it's impossible for my mind to not begin to fear that history is repeating itself. A young woman lost her life here in the past and what if it is happening again? Or what if it's already done and I'm too late to save my child, just like Paisley's parents were too late to save theirs?

I don't want to be them, full of regret and sadness, but also desperation.

A desperation to know the truth.

The truth of who took the most precious person from them.

'Bonnie!' I call out, my voice piercing through the tall trees that stand silently all around me, trees that are holding onto their secrets, never sharing what they may have seen happen here over the years.

This place is cursed. It has to be.

But not today. Please, not today.

Let today be a day when everything is OK.

'Bonnie!' I try again as I press on, still scouring every inch of these woods for a sighting of my daughter somewhere. If she was here, she would surely have heard me by now and called back, right?

Only if she is still alive.

I feel sick and, more than that, I feel alone. Not only am I without Bonnie, but I'm without the rest of my family too and I feel powerless, as if I am only strong when my loved ones are near. I also feel stupid because it was me who made us come here. My husband warned me about this place. He said it wasn't worth it. He left here when he was young, and everything was fine. I made him come back and now I'm afraid that by the time I get to leave, I'll have lost something that cannot be replaced.

I know Bonnie could just be talking to that guy, or maybe she's kissing him. It's not the end of the world if she is. Based on what happened here, I am imagining her being hurt, as if every young woman who finds herself alone with a man here will be hurt too. But if it could happen to Paisley, why can't it happen to Bonnie?

I felt somebody watching me and my daughter earlier when we were here after our picnic. I heard them too. What if they were watching her? What if they wanted to get Bonnie alone and now they have her, it's too late?

It might have been him. The guy she was with in the pub. She could have fallen for his charms, but he might not be a good guy. Any woman is capable of being misled by a clever man.

I understand Paisley's mother now; how she could have allowed something so bad to happen. It's because it's not her fault. A parent can't control their teenage daughter, not when they start showing an interest in members of the opposite sex and have a wish to do more grown-up things, away from the watchful eyes of their parents. Anything can happen then. We hope it's good, but it could be bad.

These woods make me think that it is bad.

I'm struggling to think about what I will say to Lachlan if he gets back to this village only to learn that his daughter is missing or hurt. I'm also worrying what I will say to William if he can't see his sister again. Then, as I reach the spot in the woods where Paisley was killed, I see something lying on the ground, something that I recognise as the jacket my daughter was wearing earlier today, and my heart skips a beat as I fear it is now on the body of my daughter.

I tentatively step towards it, but as I get closer, I see it is only her jacket and she is not with it. So where is my daughter? What has happened to her? Has she come to harm? Am I too late to help her?

'Mum?'

I spin around and see Bonnie standing behind me looking very confused.

'What are you doing here?' she asks me as if I'm the one in the wrong and not her for sneaking off without telling me where she was going.

'You're OK?' I ask breathlessly as my eyes scan her for any visible injuries, of which there appear to be none.

'Yeah, I'm fine,' she says. 'Are you?'

I must not look fine if my daughter is asking, and I guess I am a little dishevelled after running around these woods for the last half an hour looking for her.

'You lied to me! You didn't go to the shop. You were here with a boy,' I say, and Bonnie doesn't deny it.

'I'm sorry,' she says, and she does actually look apologetic about it.

'What were you thinking? I've been worried sick waiting for you to return!' I cry.

'It was stupid. I shouldn't have done it. I just wanted to see him, so we came here, to hang out. But it was a waste of time because he left when he realised I wasn't going to do anything with him.'

'Nothing happened?'

'No, nothing. Well, apart from me leaving my jacket behind,' Bonnie says as she picks it up off the floor. 'I forgot this, so I came back. I was on my way back to the pub. I didn't know you were out here looking for me.'

It might have been a little overdramatic of me to be running around and jumping to conclusions, but rather that than not care, and I'm just relieved now that Bonnie is safe and well.

'Seriously, what did you think had happened to me?' she asks, laughing.

'I don't know. I guess the whole Paisley thing, and what happened here before. I was worried.'

'There's no need to be. I can look after myself,' Bonnie tells me, and that's good to know, although I wonder if Paisley thought the same thing before her demise.

'Let's get out of here,' I say, walking in what I now know is the correct direction back to the village, so there will be no repeat of us getting lost like earlier.

Bonnie walks alongside me and by the time the two of us are back in the village, out from under the tree canopy in the woods and back in the full rays of the sun, my daughter checks her phone and tells me she has a message.

'It's bro. He says he and Dad are on the way back.'

I frown as I check my watch.

'That's early. The festival can't have finished already.'

'Maybe it got cancelled,' Bonnie says with a shrug. 'Or maybe it was boring. I did tell him it would be. Who goes to a festival where there's no alcohol?'

Bonnie chuckles to herself at her sibling's problems, but I'm not so convinced that's the reason he and Lachlan are on their way back.

What if something else has happened? What if returning early is more my husband's idea than my son's?

What if something else is going on?

I guess I won't know for sure until I see Lachlan and ask him.

But will he tell me the truth?

THIRTY-FIVE

LACHLAN

'Dad, seriously, slow down.'

I glance at my son beside me and see that he is anxiously looking at the road ahead. Then I notice that he's gripping the seats, and while it's not quite tight enough for his knuckles to turn white, I have a feeling that might be what happens next if I increase my speed any more. My son didn't seem to have a problem, or even notice, when I was a little over the speed limit on the motorway as I drove us back to Scotland. But as time has gone on, my foot has grown a little heavier on the accelerator pedal, no doubt a result of me being aware that every minute that ticks by is a minute where it's more likely that the police are looking for me. That must be why I've reached a speed where my son, someone who probably thinks it's quite cool to be in a fast car, is now aware that this is not fun at all.

It's dangerous. Reckless. And he wants it to stop.

'Ooops, didn't realise quite how fast I was going then,' I say, trying to sound like it was an innocent mistake as I ease off and my speed reduces naturally, though I'm still racing along.

It's been a few hours now since I collected William from the festival, my task of getting him to come with me made much easier by the fact he had his heart broken by a girl he liked and so was in a vulnerable state when I found him. That has helped me make good time and we're already back in Scotland and only a few miles away from Carnfield now. But it doesn't mean I can relax and slow down too much because the news must be spreading fast that I'm a wanted man, and the police search will be growing wider by the second, which means they could catch up with me eventually. So I must keep on pushing, trying to stay ahead, all the while trying to figure out what I can do to keep my family together.

'Don't worry, I won't tell Mum,' William says with a smile to let me know that he won't be getting me in trouble for driving too fast. But while it's an innocent comment from his point of view, it only makes me feel worse. All I am thinking is the fact that at some point, somebody will tell my wife what I have done. I don't mean the speeding, I mean the murders, or in Francesca's case, the attempted murder. Even if I'm somehow able to get away with what I did years ago with Paisley and Teri, there is no way I can talk myself out of what happened today. Jenny will learn to her horror who I really am eventually and there'll be no way back for me and her then. There'll also be no way back for me with the kids because she'll obviously want to separate me from them, ensuring their safety and punishing me for the bad things I have done while sharing a home with them all. The police will have a punishment of their own planned too, but strangely, multiple years locked up in a cell doesn't seem as bad as being separated from my loved ones and that's when I realise that whatever happens, I cannot go on without them.

Jenny. Bonnie. William.

If I can't have them, no one can.

I realise what it is that I'm thinking then. The gravity of it. The horror of it. The sheer desperation of it.

It's unspeakable, but crucially, frighteningly, it's not impossible.

For a man capable of taking lives, what are three more, along with my own, if it's the only way to ensure I stay with my family forever?

I make sure to keep my eyes on the road ahead, not only because I'm still driving fast and don't want to miss the turn-off to Carnfield but also because I can't bear to see my son's face at this time. Not when I'm contemplating his life, and his sister's, and his mother's. He doesn't know it. Neither do they. But behind the familiar face of their father is a darkness that may soon consume them all.

I hit the brakes when I see the turning up ahead and manage to make it, though I'm still going a little faster than I should be, and William laughs nervously because he knows it as well as I do.

'You should have been a racing car driver,' William jests, and I smile, but it hides all my pain.

I should have been something different. Anything but the person I have become. Now it's too late and I can't undo it. People can change their careers, but they can't change their personality. I'm no racing car driver. I'm a serial killer. Up until today, I was a very successful one. I've just suffered a very large setback and now I'm like most other serial killers who came before me.

I'm the serial killer who got caught.

We speed into Carnfield, and the tyres squeal as I bring us to a stop outside the pub. I'm hoping Jenny and Bonnie are in the room so I can get them to gather their things together quickly and we can be on the move again, but I won't know for sure until I get upstairs.

'Seriously, how much caffeine did you have while I was at the festival?' William asks me as I take the staircase two steps at a time, but I ignore him and burst into the room, grateful when I see that my wife and daughter are in here.

'You're back early,' Jenny says, stating the obvious but

sounding sceptical. 'What happened? Did you make it to the festival?'

'Yeah,' William says as he enters the room behind me, but I'm already busy packing, grabbing everything in sight and throwing it into our suitcases so there is less chance of a delay.

'What's going on?' Bonnie asks. 'Are we leaving now?'

'Yes, we are,' I say as I keep packing. 'Come on, let's go.'

But nobody moves, not because they're lazy but because they don't possess the need for urgency like I do and can, therefore, be slow and complacent.

Oh, to have the luxury of innocence.

'Where are we going?' Jenny asks, and I need a quick and good answer for that.

'I've booked us a cabin out in the countryside,' I say as I continue to pack. 'Got a last-minute deal. I thought we could finish our holiday off there.'

That sounds plausible, and once I've said it, William starts packing, which is a sign of progress. Maybe he's being so compliant because I supported him during his time of need back at the festival, but whatever the reason, he is making moves to leave here, so it's just my wife and daughter to work on now. But as always, the females in my family require a little more convincing.

'What cabin?' Bonnie enquires.

'I found it online. It looks great. Very luxurious. There's even a hot tub,' I say, and those seem to be the magic words that get Bonnie moving.

That just leaves my wife to conquer now and she's always the toughest nut to crack.

'Where is it?' Jenny asks.

'Huh?' I say as I keep packing like a madman.

'This cabin you've spontaneously booked for us all. Where is it? What's the address?'

'It's up north. It's remote. But I've got directions. Let's get going now so we're there before dark.'

I zip up my suitcase then and haul it to the door where I put it down because that's ready to go. Now to get my wife's things, and it would be really great if she helped me gather them up, but she's still querying this plan.

'Why didn't you consult with me?' she asks.

'I thought it would be a nice surprise,' I reply, starting on her packing for her.

'Since when do you do surprises?'

'I thought you'd like the idea of it,' I say, wondering if I can make her feel guilty and that will have her stop questioning me and show a bit of gratitude towards my idea.

Of course, the cabin is fictitious, so I'm not seeking gratitude. I'm simply seeking a way for me and my family to be in the car and on the move again so we can get to a place where there is no phone signal, and they can't read about the search for me online. Then, once there, I can do what I need to do next. But not before. It won't work before.

'Come on, Mum, let's get out of here,' Williams urges, and Bonnie agrees.

'Yeah, I want to go in the hot tub,' she says, blissfully unaware there is no such thing awaiting us.

The kids are almost packed up now, and as I throw more of Jenny's things into her suitcase, we'll all be ready to go very soon. Recognising that she is the only one holding up the entire family now, Jenny gets to her feet and joins in with the packing. But as she does, I notice her look at me a few times, and while she isn't saying anything, the expression on her face suggests she is trying to figure something out.

She's trying to work out whether I am telling the truth and that's because she wants to know if she should trust me.

Hopefully, she'll guess wrong.

If so, it doesn't matter if she realises her mistake later.

It'll be too late for her by then.

THIRTY-SIX
JENNY

No one likes to be rushed, but this is going too far. It's one thing for Lachlan to tell us to pack quickly so we can go to some cabin he says he's booked, but to get us to leave without thanking the people who let us stay in the spare room above the pub? That won't do. I have better manners than that, which is why I'm trying to find somebody in the pub so I can say thank you and let them know we are leaving now. But Lachlan isn't happy.

'You don't need to thank them. They knew we were leaving today, so let's just go,' he says, with Bonnie and William, and all our bags, already in the car outside, which means it's only me who needs to get in so he can drive off.

'It'll only take a second,' I say, which I expect it will, but that seems to be a second too long for my husband and I'm now starting to get very concerned. He's acting impulsively, impatiently, as if he is anxious about something and needs to get out of here as quickly as possible. Then there's the fact he and William came back much earlier than expected and I still don't know why because Lachlan won't tell me. This behaviour, coupled with his strange demeanour when he first arrived here and crashed our car, and mixed in with what Angus said about him suspecting Lachlan, makes for a cocktail that has me on my guard.

It's not nice to have to be wary around my husband.

But I'm afraid he's leaving me with no choice.

'I'll be in the car,' Lachlan says when he realises that I'm really not going to go until I have thanked the pub owner, so he leaves me in here by myself. No sooner has he gone than the woman who offered us the room appears.

'Checking out?' she asks, and I confirm that we are, handing her back the key to the room.

'Thanks so much for sorting that out for us.'

'No problem. So, where are you off to next?'

'That's a good question. I'm not sure, exactly,' I reply, which seems absurd, but it's the truth. I have no idea where this cabin is that Lachlan is so set on taking us to.

'Well, wherever it is, have a good time. Will we be seeing you guys again?'

'Possibly,' I say, feeling bad if I say no, but I can't imagine ever needing to come back here.

'I hope Lachlan has said his goodbyes this time,' she says then before I can leave. 'Not like last time. He just went without so much as a goodbye to anyone and no one really knew why. Some thought he must have had an argument with his parents, but if he did, they never admitted it. They were a bit of a strange family, by all accounts.'

I pause as I think about that. I knew my husband left here as a youngster. But he didn't say goodbye to anyone? He must have been really desperate to leave back then. Just like he's desperate to leave now.

The question is, what causes this desperation?

I thank the woman one more time before stepping out of the pub to find Lachlan behind the wheel of the car, the kids in the back and the engine running. He looks like a racing car driver on the starting grid of a big race, eager to get the green light so he can hit the accelerator pedal and speed away. But unlike those people, whose job it is to be fast, my husband does not need to be so eager.

Unless there is something wrong.

I get in the car, taking my place on the passenger seat, still very wary of the man seated next to me, who has us moving before I've even got my seatbelt on properly. I look back at the kids to make sure they are okay, but they both seem fine, heads down, eyes on their phones, behaving normally.

So it's just Lachlan who is being weird.

'So, where is this place? You can tell us now, right?' I ask as we leave the village.

'We'll be there soon enough,' Lachlan replies, driving a little fast, and I look over to see the speedometer steadily increasing.

'How long are we staying for? We're still going home tomorrow, aren't we?' I check. 'Because the kids need to be back, and you have work.'

'Of course,' Lachlan replies, but he sounds very distracted, as if his answer was just to please me, not because it's the truth.

'Slow down a little bit,' I say.

'Just relax,' he tells me.

'You're going too fast.'

'It's fine.'

I really don't like this. Something is going on and I need to know what it is. But how can I find out if he won't tell me?

'Watch out!' I cry as we round a bend, and Lachlan swerves the car just in time before we hit the person walking by the side of the road. But he doesn't slow down to check if they are okay, so it's only because I glance in the rear-view mirror that I see who it was.

It was Angus and his bag of beer cans, the bag now on the floor and the cans rolling around on the road after he narrowly avoided being struck by our car. I don't know why he is walking out here, and Lachlan clearly didn't expect to see him or anyone else out on the road, but the fact is he almost hit him.

I look at my husband, figuring such a surprise like that might be the thing to get him to realise he is rushing too much and finally slow down. But it's had the opposite effect. He seems to be going even faster now, and not only that, but he is sweating.

Something is really bothering him, which means it's bothering me and because our children are in the car with us, I have to think about what is best for them.

Right now, I feel like the best thing is for us to not be here, in this car, speeding through the countryside. That's why, as I look at the fields and the trees whizzing by my window in a green blur, I decide to try something.

'Stop the car. I need a toilet break,' I say, using that as the excuse that will hopefully get this car to stop.

'What?' Lachlan says, not following orders yet.

'I said stop the car. I really need to go.'

'But we've only just set off!'

'You didn't give me the chance to go to the toilet before we left, so I have to go now. Pull over and I'll go in these trees,' I say, gesturing to the forest up ahead.

Lachlan is still driving fast, and I wonder if there's going to have to be a repeat of what happened earlier between us when he grabbed the wheel and forced me off the road. It really would be a déjà vu moment if I have to do the same to him. But I'm not going to risk an accident, so I will keep using only my words, rather than force.

'Stop this car right now!' I shout at the top of my voice, and as the kids lift their heads up from their phones and look at me in shock, I see Lachlan do the same. Then he does as I say, bringing the car to a stop.

'Thank you,' I tell him before opening my door.

'Be quick,' he says. 'The sun is setting, and we still have a bit of a drive ahead of us.'

I'm not being rushed as I get out, nor do I intend on getting back in the car and now all I need to do is make sure Bonnie and William get out too.

'Why don't you two take a toilet break as well?' I suggest. 'None of us went before setting off and it could be a long drive yet like your father says.'

I use Lachlan's words against him, and Bonnie takes the opportunity to do as I suggest, but William seems happy to stay in the car, which is not what I want. And Lachlan doesn't want anybody getting out at all.

'There's no need for stretching your legs. We'll be there soon if we can just keep going,' he says, but I ignore him and look to William.

'Hey, can you come and look at this?' I ask my son.

'What is it?' he asks.

'Just get out,' I say, and I'm relieved he is able to without Lachlan realising something is wrong and locking the doors.

Now that all three of us are out of the car and it's only Lachlan inside it, I can breathe a momentary sigh of relief. But it is only momentary because we're still standing out here in the middle of nowhere and I still don't know what has got my husband so spooked.

It must be something that happened back home, as he's been acting crazy ever since returning from taking William to the festival.

I don't know. All I do know is that I'm not getting back in his car, so as I walk towards the trees, making it seem to my husband like I am going to take an impromptu toilet stop in the wild, I tell my children to come with me.

Thankfully, they listen and we head into the woods.

And gratefully, Lachlan is still in the car which means he doesn't know we're not going to rejoin him.

Not yet, anyway.

THIRTY-SEVEN

LACHLAN

I impatiently drum my fingers on the steering wheel while checking the digital clock on my dashboard. We're burning time, time I do not have, and I cannot wait to get moving again. I've left the engine running because that will speed things up when my family get back in the car, but the problem is, they are still out of it.

I turn and look through the passenger side window but can't see anybody now. Where did they all go?

Jenny needed to take a personal break, so I guess she has gone deeper into the trees at the side of the road to find somewhere more private in case a motorist passes by and sees her. But while that's understandable, it's frustrating that the kids went to do the same, something that seems unnecessary as we've not long left the village, but Jenny suggested it and they went for it.

I suppose this might be my fault. I haven't told them exactly how long the drive is to get to the cabin, so they are probably thinking they'll take this opportunity for a rest stop in case it's hours until we get there. The only reason I haven't told them how far there is to go is because the cabin doesn't exist.

My plan, the one they cannot know about yet, is to keep driving, away from everyone and everything, to a place where we have the time and space to try and figure this out. Maybe, if I can convince Jenny that the only way for us to survive as a family is for us to keep going and never look back, she will stick with me. The kids too.

If not, there is no future for any of us.

Another minute ticks by, another wasted minute, and the thought of the police out there being active while I'm sitting here being so passive is driving me mad. I want to get out and get my family back in the car, but just before I do that, I decide to check the news on my phone and see if I have made head-lines yet.

I just about have enough signal strength on my mobile, but that won't last long the further we get into the wilderness, so I better take this opportunity now.

As I navigate to the news, I wonder how many people in the world have ever been in this very unusual position that I find myself in now. How many people have ever checked the news to see if they are in it for committing a crime? It feels bizarre, almost surreal, but this is my reality, one I can only blame myself for, and as the page for my local newspaper site loads up on my screen, I hold my breath.

Then I see it. Right there in black, bold writing.

It's my name, followed by the words,

MANHUNT UNDERWAY FOR ATTEMPTED MURDER

This is conclusive proof that not only has Francesca already spoken to the police, but that the police have released the infor-mation to the wider public so they can be on the lookout for me. *They have also been warned to stay away from me because I'm a dangerous man.*

There is no photo yet, no image of me to accompany the dramatic headline, but I guess it's only a matter of time until that changes. The police will get their hands on my image, it's in the public's interest to do so, and then there will be no doubt among the people who know me back home that I am the one being sought in connection with this crime. As shocking as the headline is, the attempted murder I am wanted for is not even the worst thing I have done, but at least all that has not come out yet and the only way it will do will be if I am caught and I confess to it.

But if I'm dead before the police get to me?

In that case, they might suspect I had something to do with Paisley's and Teri's murders.

But they'll never know for sure.

I'm not one of these killers who wants everyone to know about all of their victims so they can take credit for them, like there's some kind of pride and prestige attached to it. I always wanted to be one of those killers who no one even knew existed. Sadly, that's gone now, but still, I'm not eager to have everything I've ever done wrong broadcast for all the world to read about. It won't be long until the national news picks up this story which is currently circulating locally, and there is no doubt about it.

Things are going to get wild very fast.

I put my phone away. I've seen enough. Now, all I want to see are my family members walking back to the car. But there is still no sign of them, so I get out of my vehicle and go in search.

I enter the treeline roughly in the area where I saw them all moving towards, expecting to find them relatively near once I do. But as I step through the trees and lose sight of the road temporarily, all I see is more trees.

I cannot see my family.

Then I realise why.

They've gone.

THIRTY-EIGHT
JENNY

It's not easy to run through thick foliage, trying to stay on your feet and avoid trip hazards like tree stumps, fallen branches and protruding plants that can tangle around your legs and slow you down. It's even harder when you don't know where you are running to and how far you are going to have to go to get away. The hardest part of all is running because you think you are in danger.

That's why my children and I are running now, putting distance between ourselves and Lachlan, who is hopefully still oblivious to what we are doing, and is still sitting in his car waiting for us to return. But we are not going to return, not because I know for sure that he poses a danger to us, but because I cannot rule it out at this stage. All I do know is that something is seriously wrong with him, and I need to get my children away from him.

I know why I am running – I got the sense that there is something seriously wrong with my husband – but as for Bonnie and William, they took a little more convincing. Unfortunately, I didn't have much time to spend standing around and talking them through everything I felt might be wrong, so I had to be quick.

'Your father is not well and we need to get him help,' I said shortly after we had all left the car and gone into the trees. 'But we need to stay away from him until then because it's dangerous.'

'What?' Bonnie and William had cried in frightened unison.

'Listen to me. You have to trust me. He's not himself. You can see that with how he's driving. He's speeding and putting us in danger and now he wants to take us to a remote cabin but he won't tell us where it is. There's something wrong and we need to find out what it is, but until we do, we need to look after each other. Okay?'

Bonnie and William had shared a nervous glance then, but there must have been enough persuasion in my voice for them to realise that I was being totally honest with them, as they listened to me and then we started moving. Or maybe it was just the fact that they had seen enough erratic behaviour from their father over the past couple of days to realise that I was right and their dad was hiding something.

We moved quickly but we only broke into a run when we heard Lachlan calling out our names, a sure sign that he had realised we had left him, and he was now trying to locate us.

'Mum, this is crazy!' Bonnie cries as we push on, and while I can still hear my husband calling my name, he seems quite far away, which means we are doing a good job of escaping. But our job will get harder if Bonnie's loud voice alerts him to our location.

'Just keep going and stay quiet. Come on,' I say, forging on through this forest we find ourselves in after abandoning the roadside.

I don't know where these trees end and what will be on the other side of them. Will we make it back to Carnfield? Some other village? Find a road possibly and flag down a passing motorist? Or will we get lost out here and struggle to find any way out? I don't know the answers, but I do know I'd rather be in this situation than be in that speeding car having Lachlan driving us somewhere unknown.

'If there's something wrong with Dad, we need to help him,' William says before he trips on a stump and almost loses his footing but regains his balance.

'Yes, we will, but we need to make sure we are safe first,' I say, not paying enough attention to where I am going and running straight into a branch.

I feel the branch scratch the skin beneath my top as I run past it, but while it stings, it's not enough to get me to stop. But when William actually falls over, Bonnie pauses and she bends down to make sure her brother is okay.

As I stop and wait for them, I look back the way we came, but I can't see Lachlan coming. I can't hear him either. He's out here somewhere, which means we can't hang around. But William and Bonnie seem to have done enough running.

'We're not going any further,' Bonnie says once she has helped her brother back to his feet. 'Not until you tell us what this is all about.'

'Yeah,' William says in agreement. 'This is crazy.'

'I know it is, but I'm just trying to keep us all safe,' I plead.

'From what? From Dad? Why? What has he done?' Bonnie demands to know.

'I don't know,' I have to admit, which is not helping my argument. 'I just know that I have seen a different side to him since we came here and based on what a few people have said, maybe there is a whole other side we haven't known about.'

'Is this about Paisley?' William asks. 'Do you think he had something to do with it?'

I really don't want to have this discussion with them, not

here, not anywhere, and my mind is focused when I hear Lachlan in the distance.

'Jenny! Bonnie! William! Where are you?'

To anyone else, it might simply sound like a loving dad trying to find his family. But to me, it sounds like a desperate man who was trying to trick us into going somewhere with him that we shouldn't have gone. Either way, all that matters is that hearing the call is proof that my husband is getting closer.

'We need to go. Now!' I say, trying not to be so loud as to alert Lachlan to our location, but also needing to stress the importance of my children following my orders. But before we move, Bonnie takes out her phone.

'I'll call someone,' she says. 'The police, or whoever. Somebody who can come and sort this out. Then we don't have to run and then Dad can get whatever help he needs, and we can figure this all out and—'

'Jenny! Bonnie! William!'

Lachlan's cries are closer again, and while what my daughter just said again demonstrates her sensible and compassionate side, I fear it is not the best thing we can do here.

'We need to make sure we are safe before we do anything,' I say. 'We can call someone when we are. Right now, we need to get moving again before he gets here and tries to get us back in that car.'

'I just want to know what is happening,' William says, throwing his hands up in frustration, and before I can have another go at telling them to move, Bonnie looks at her phone and I see her eyes go wide.

'What is it?' I ask her.

'I've just got a message from Melissa,' she says, and I know who that is. It's her best friend at home. But what has she said that could seem to shock my daughter so much?

'What about?' I ask her anxiously.

'She says Dad is on the news,' Bonnie replies.

'What?' William cries.

'She says he is wanted for an attempted murder today,' Bonnie adds. 'Back home.'

I can't believe that. It doesn't make sense. Lachlan tried to kill somebody in our hometown today? I don't see how that is possible. But he was there. Of course he was. He drove William back for the festival. So it is possible. But is it plausible?

'This can't be right,' Bonnie says. 'I need to check this.'

She types on her phone then and I assume she is making an internet search. A few seconds later, I get confirmation of that.

'Oh my god, it really is on the news! The police are hunting for Dad!' she cries, and I grab her phone because I have to see it for myself. It's true. It's right here in black and white. My husband is wanted in connection with an attempted murder.

'He came to get me early from the festival,' William tells us then, looking afraid. 'He never actually said why. And then he was driving really, really fast to get us back up here.'

It seems my son is connecting the dots as to why his father did those things. It sounds like he did something very, very wrong back home and now the police want him.

Maybe Angus was right. Maybe that awful feeling I have had ever since coming here is right too.

Lachlan has been hiding something.

Something terrible.

'I'll call the police,' I say as I dial three nines and put the phone to my ear. But before the call can connect, I see something that would render me speechless even if the operator answers my call in a second.

I see Lachlan in the distance and, worse than that, he sees us too.

Now he is coming right towards us.

And it feels too late to escape.

THIRTY-NINE

LACHLAN

I can see my family through the trees, all three of them standing together, as if in a tribe, while I'm here, all by myself, feeling exiled. And as human nature would have it, the people in the tribes survive while the person separated from them often perishes. But I'm determined not to perish, which is why I'm eager to join up with the rest of my family, and now I can see them, that should be able to happen.

Until they start running.

If I was holding out any hope that my wife and children weren't afraid of me and had genuinely ventured deep into this forest for some other reason, it is extinguished as I watch them fleeing. Interestingly, Jenny goes one way while Bonnie and William go the other. I guess they have decided to split up, for what reason I'm not sure, and initially, I'm also not sure who to try and chase after first.

My wife or my kids?

I figure Jenny will be easier to catch than two teenagers, so I go in her direction, but no sooner have I done that than I lose her in the dense trees. When I look back the other way, I can still just about make out Bonnie and William, so having lost my wife, I go in pursuit of them instead.

I'm able to maintain a visual on the pair of them as they run ahead of me, but whenever they look back to see where I am, I can see fear on their faces and it's an awful sight. Whatever has happened, whether it is something Jenny has said to them or something else, they look truly terrified of me now and it is breaking my heart to see them behave like this towards me.

I feel like I'm losing them, literally as well as spiritually, because they are faster than me and the gap between us is widening. But then Bonnie trips and falls flat on her face and when William stops to help her, I realise I am going to catch up with them after all.

'Stay back!' William cries as he kneels beside his sister and puts one hand out as if to try and keep me at bay. What does he think I'm going to do? Attack them? It looks that way, and as Bonnie gets to her feet, the pair of them stand together, side by side, cowering, afraid of what I might do next.

'What are you doing?' I ask them as I try to catch my breath. 'Why are you running from me?'

'You know why!' Bonnie cries, panic on her face and in her voice.

'What? No, I don't. What's going on?' I ask, needing them to tell me; otherwise, I will try and maintain my innocence until the bitter end.

'You tried to kill somebody!' William cries then. 'Today, back home, after you drove me back for the festival. Is that why you were speeding so fast back here? Because the police were looking for you?'

'What are you talking about?' I ask, but my metaphorical mask is slipping, I can feel it.

'It's in the news! Melissa told me!' Bonnie cries. 'You're wanted for attempted murder!'

I guess they have seen the same headline I did a few

moments ago in the car. That sure does explain why they would be so desperate to get away from me. So how can I rescue this situation? Or is it over?

'Guys, listen to me. I can explain,' I begin, figuring if I can only buy myself a little more time, and perhaps come up with some kind of story that might make me seem less of a deranged psychopath, maybe they will still love me, and I won't have to take drastic measures to stop them getting away from me forever.

'Tell it to the police!' Bonnie cries. 'Just stay away from us!'

'Have you called them?' I ask nervously then before looking around as if there might be several officers in uniform coming towards me from all sides.

'Yes! We have!' William cries, but that seemed too enthusiastic, so I get the sense he is bluffing. That's good. Maybe I have more time than I think. I need to calm them both down. I also need to find where Jenny went.

Then I hear a noise behind me and turn around and, sure enough, it's my wife.

She's come back. Now the four of us are together again. So maybe there is a way out of this...

But I fail to see the thick branch Jenny is holding in her hand until it is too late.

She strikes me in the face with it hard.

That's when I fall to the ground and everything goes black.

FORTY

JENNY

'Run to the car! Go!' I tell my children, and such is the ferocity of my command, both of them obey it instantly and take off running in the direction we just spent time coming from. While they do that, I look down at the man lying by my feet.

Lachlan appears to be unconscious, which is a relief. I now know that when he is awake, he is very, very dangerous. While he is like this, he cannot hurt me or anyone else. But I can't relax yet, not until he is in custody and the police can resolve whatever it is he has done, while me, Bonnie and William watch safely from afar.

This man I just knocked out by hitting him over the head with a tree branch.

This man I used to love.

This man I call my husband.

I take out my phone and make a call, grateful I have a signal here to connect me to the police, like I'm grateful that my daughter had a signal so she could receive the message from her best friend alerting her to the fact that Lachlan was wanted for attempted murder.

'Hello? Yes, I need the police, immediately!' I cry when my call is answered. 'I'm in a forest about ten minutes outside Carnfield in Scotland. I don't know my exact location, but I'm not too far from the main road and my husband's car is parked there. You'll see it if you come. And there will be two teenagers standing with it. They are my children. I've told them to wait there while I stay with my husband. I just knocked him unconscious because he's the one you're looking for. Lachlan Ferguson. He's the one you want for——'

The phone suddenly flies out of my hand as I fall backwards and when I land, I find myself staring up at the treetops and the darkening sky above them.

What just happened?

I get my answer when I look down and see Lachlan with a hand around one of my ankles.

He just pulled me to the floor.

He's awake.

'Get off me!' I shout as I try to release my leg from his grip, but he keeps a tight hold on me, so I give up on trying to break free of him and go in search of the mobile phone. I'm hoping it's still connected to the police, but I won't know for sure unless I find it and check.

'Get off!' I cry again before I spot the device lying on the forest floor just out of reach of where I lie and while I desperately try to grab it, Lachlan is pulling me in the opposite direction.

I look towards him and see the blood pouring from his head where I struck him. But it wasn't a fatal blow, nor was it seemingly one that could keep him unconscious for more than a few minutes, and now it's no longer Lachlan who is in big trouble, but me.

He scrambles towards me and seems intent on pinning me down beneath him, but as he rises up my body, I instinctively raise my knee to fend him off and it strikes him directly between his legs.

He groans and rolls off me and I take my chance to scramble to my feet and grab the phone before I start running, though in my haste to escape my husband's clutches, I realise I am running in the opposite direction to the road.

Rather than heading back to safety, I'm now heading deeper into this forest, but I can't turn back now because Lachlan is already on his feet and in pursuit, so I keep going.

Leaping over fallen logs and darting between drooping trees, I take a risk by momentarily lowering my eyes from the cluttered pathway ahead to look at my phone's screen. When I do, I see that the call to the police has disconnected, so I just have to hope that they heard enough from me to understand the severity of the situation and locate where I am.

As I run, I realise that when I spoke to them, I told them my husband was unconscious, so at that point, there was no immediate threat to my life. That might affect their response time, but that has changed now, and my life is seemingly very much under threat, so am I going to be able to fend Lachlan off until the police get here?

I tell myself that the police will be quick. I made sure to give them his name and that's a name that is in the news now, so that should add urgency to their response.

'Where are you going?' Lachlan calls after me, but I don't turn back. 'Do you really think you can get away from me?'

I am scared to answer that, not only because slowing down to do so might mean he catches me, but also because I'm afraid he is confident he will be able to stop me, and all this running is going to be in vain.

'What did you do?' I call after him as I keep sprinting. 'Who did you hurt?'

Unsurprisingly, Lachlan doesn't answer my questions either. He continues his pursuit, doggedly coming after me, as if catching me could somehow make all of this better. But it can't. He has to know it's over for him and whatever secrets he has are unravelling in full public view.

So why isn't he giving up and leaving me alone?

'Argh!' I cry as I wrap my hands around a leaning tree trunk and hold on tight, as that's the only thing that has prevented me from going over the edge of a large drop.

I had failed to see the ground falling away until the last second, but luckily I did; otherwise, I would have gone right over and rolled down this steep embankment, potentially breaking a few bones along the way and hitting the water at the bottom. I can see the blue waters of a loch down there. But I've been able to stop, and while that has kept me safe in the short term, it only means one thing in the long term.

Still gripping the tree trunk, I tentatively turn around and, when I do, I see my husband has stopped running and is slowly walking towards me instead. He has obviously seen that he has me cornered and doesn't feel the need to rush anymore.

'Stay back!' I warn him, though given our current positions, I am the one who seems more in danger, not him.

'Relax. Calm down. I just want to talk,' Lachlan says. 'Come away from the edge. It's okay. I won't hurt you.'

'How do I know that?' I scream at him.

'Because you're my wife,' he says, as if that gives me some kind of immunity to his threat. But does it? Is he serious that he wouldn't harm me because we're married? Or is he trying to lull me into a false sense of security so I lower my guard and then he can strike?

'Tell me what you did!' I demand to know, still holding onto the tree as if it's a person who can protect me from Lachlan. 'Why are you wanted for attempted murder?'

'I can explain,' Lachlan says, taking a few more steps towards me.

'Then explain!'

Lachlan stops approaching me and it's as if a sense of calm permeates the area. He looks at peace, like he's finally about to shed the cloak he has been wearing throughout our marriage and is now ready to reveal his true self.

'There's something wrong with me,' he says as I continue to teeter on the edge. 'I noticed it when I was a teenager. Around William's age. I noticed it when I first started being interested in girls.'

Lachlan looks at me, seeing that I'm terrified yet still preferring to hug the tree over him, and he shakes his head before going on.

'I get jealous. No, it's more than that. I can't stand to see someone I like with someone else. Not just someone else, but someone I know. The two of them together, it feels like they're rubbing my face in it. I know they're not, but that's how it feels to me, so what am I supposed to do?'

'What have you done?' I ask, my voice a whisper, but it's audible because all the birds in this area of the forest seem to have stopped singing, as if they have either had the smarts to leave already or are hiding in silence as the threat exists below them.

'I was envious of Angus being with Paisley,' Lachlan admits. 'That's why I had the fight with him and that's why I followed them into the woods that night. I was spying on them. It was torture, but I had to see. That's how I saw that they had an argument, and he left. Paisley was by herself. She spotted me, so I had no choice but to approach her. I thought, maybe, she might see that I was better than Angus. That maybe there was a chance something could happen between us two. But no...'

Lachlan's voice trails off, and I'm grateful it does because I can fill in the blanks.

'You killed her,' I say, not a question, simply a very, very sad statement and my husband nods, admitting to murder, not in a court of law but to me, which is just as devastating.

'How could you live with yourself?' I ask him, needing the tree more than ever for support. 'How could you go all this time with the secret of what you had done? Her poor parents. The police investigation. Innocent people being accused. How could you do it? How could you marry me and have a career and raise children with all that going on in your head?'

'I don't know,' Lachlan admits. 'Like I said, there is something wrong with me.'

'What happened today?' I ask. 'What did you do today?'

'I went to a colleague's home.'

'What's her name?' I ask, like a wife who has found out her husband is cheating on her, but rather than wanting to know which woman he has been trying to sleep with, I'm finding out which woman he tried to kill.

'Francesca.'

'So, what happened? You liked her, but she didn't like you? She liked someone else? Just like Paisley? Is that it?'

Lachlan says nothing, which is as good as a yes.

'What is wrong with you? You can't kill people simply because they don't want to be with you!'

'I didn't kill her. She's alive,' he says, as if that makes him a better person.

'She's gone to the police,' I say, referring to the news articles about the search for him, and he sadly nods.

'It's over,' he admits. 'I don't know what to do.'

'This cabin,' I say. 'Does it even exist?'

Lachlan shakes his head.

'I just wanted to take you all somewhere quiet. Where we could be a family. One last time.'

If I didn't know it already, getting myself and the kids out of that car was one of the best decisions I've ever made and I'm grateful to my intuition.

'You need to go to the police and hand yourself in,' I tell Lachlan, who looks incredibly weak as I say it. 'Admit what you have done and tell them you need help, and they will get that help for you. Nobody else has to get hurt. Things can get better.'

'I'll still have to go to prison,' he says mournfully. 'For the people I have killed.'

'You were technically a child when you killed Paisley, so maybe your sentence won't be as long,' I say, simply trying to come up with things to say that will get him to give up quicker so I am safe.

'But I'm not a child now, am I?' he says, looking at me. 'I wasn't a child when I tried to kill Francesca. And I wasn't a child when I murdered Teri.'

I almost lose my grip on the tree trunk then because as shocking as what he has been saying has been for me, I hadn't pieced this last part of it together.

The part where he could be the man responsible for the death of my best friend.

'No,' is all I can muster, tears in my eyes as I realise the man who held me during all the nights I cried after Teri's death, and during her funeral itself, is the same man who took her from me.

'I'm sorry,' Lachlan says, as if that makes it forgivable.

I feel sick. I need to run. I need to get away from him. If the police aren't here to remove him from my sight, I'll have to do it myself. But how can I get past him? He's blocking the way. I can't go backwards because of this steep drop. What can I do? Then Lachlan steps towards me and makes my mind up for me.

'Don't you see, Jenny?' he says, a menacing tone to his voice. 'I don't like it when other men have what I can't. If I go to prison, someone else might have you one day. I can't allow that. If I can't have you, no one can.'

As he gets closer, I realise what this means. He is going to kill me before he lets the police get him. Or maybe he will hurt himself too. And the kids? It's a terrifying possibility.

That's why I have to fight back.

I let go of the tree, and while Lachlan expects me to try and run past him, I wait for him to reach me.

Then, just before he can push me over the edge, I wrap my arms around him and drag him over with me.

FORTY-ONE

JENNY

The whole world is spinning, and I see flashes of the sky mixed in with flashes of the steep slope my husband and I are falling down.

I'm doing my best to tuck into a position where my head might be saved from hitting any hard objects, as well as hopefully reducing my chances of suffering a broken bone. But the reality is that I'm totally out of control, falling, falling, falling, and until I stop, I won't know what the damage is.

Lachlan is falling with me, and I can hear his cries of pain as he hits various things on his way down to the bottom, telling me he might not be doing as good a job as me at shielding himself from potential hazards. I was prepared for this fall, at least partly, because I instigated it. But Lachlan had no idea that I was about to drag both of us over the edge, not until it was too late, which is what it is now.

I feel something hard hit my right hip and let out a cry of pain, but whatever it was, it doesn't break my fall and I continue to tumble down until eventually, mercifully, I come to a stop. When I do, it takes me a few seconds to get my bearings and even longer to get my breath back. As I look up at the sky and then at the edge of the loch beside me that I almost went into, I try to move my body and feel sore but not broken. That tells me I might be able to get up and get out of here.

But what about my husband?

I look to my right but don't see him, so slowly turn my head to the left, my neck aching as I do, and that's when I spot him. He's lying on his back, his body partially in the water but his face above it, his mouth open and his eyes closed. He looks unconscious, but this happened before and he shocked me by waking up, so I'm not going to take any chances this time.

I get to my feet as quickly as I can and then look around for a weapon, just in case.

I see a large rock and pick it up, feeling the weight of it in my hands and hoping I don't have to use it but feeling like it's more than strong enough for the job if I do. This is how Paisley died, I think to myself, or rather, this is how my husband killed her.

Strong blows to the head with a rock.

That's what the documentary said was her cause of death.

Will it also be my husband's?

I stand over him, the rock in my hands, waiting to have to use it, though I don't wish to because that would make me a killer too. But he still doesn't move and only after a few minutes do I relax and lower it before eventually dropping it, hearing the loud thud it makes as it hits the ground. Then I look around, trying to figure out how to get out of here because I doubt I'll be able to climb back up the embankment. I might have to, though, as we're on the banks of this loch, a very scenic one, with a view of the mountains on the other side of it, but one that makes me feel trapped now. The tranquillity of it is spoilt by what just happened, the shocking revelations that my husband made, as well as the fact I would rather have risked serious injury or even death by dragging him down this steep slope, to keep my children safe at the top of it.

I think about Bonnie and William, how they have hopefully found their way back to the road and are waiting for me by the car. But they won't know if I'm okay, so they must be worried, which means I need to get to them as quickly as possible. That's why I turn away from the loch and prepare to find a route that takes me back to them. But as I do, I see Lachlan, and he's not where I left him.

He's back on his feet.

And he's picked up the rock I was holding.

'Wait!' I try, desperately putting my hands out in front of myself as I move backwards, my feet entering the water, but I don't care about that because I'm just trying to get away from him before he can hit me. I made a mistake assuming he was already dead or at least unconscious, and I certainly made a mistake dropping my weapon. But that realisation doesn't help me much as Lachlan follows me into the water, and as he raises the rock above his head, I don't have the time or the space to get out of the trajectory of his blow. That's until Lachlan stumbles on something beneath the water, losing his footing for a split-second, and as he goes off balance, he lets go of the rock.

It hits the surface of the loch, sending large ripples out across the water in all directions, but before it completely sinks to the bottom, I reach down and scoop it up. Then, as my husband continues to try and get his balance, I bring the rock down hard on his head, hearing the sickening crunch as it impacts his skull.

I see the whites of Lachlan's eyes as he falls backwards, his entire body in the water now, but I only see them for a second before he goes under, his body creating deep ripples in the loch's surface as he crashes through it.

As I whirl around, desperate to get out of the water, I only serve to create even more ripples and while I want to wait to see if he breaks back up through the surface, a stronger part of me wants to run and find the children. My maternal instincts win out so I turn and flee, figuring I can at least get a good head start on my husband if he does remerge. But by the time I have climbed and scrambled my way back to the top of the embankment, I haven't heard him call after me. When I allow myself to look back at the loch, I see the surface is calm. No ripples in the water suggest no signs of life beneath it. That means he must be dead.

Is this nightmare finally over?

FORTY-TWO

JENNY

It should feel like something is missing in our house now that there is one less person living here. Usually, the loss of a family member would mean change, and upheaval, and a hole being left that feels like it can never be filled. But that's not the case here. If anything, it feels like the surviving members of this family had a very lucky escape.

It's been a month now since I discovered Lachlan's dark past. A month since I learnt of the true horror that was inside the man I married, the same man who I thought made an excellent father and husband. And a month since I last saw him with my own eyes, the second before he slipped beneath the water after I had killed him before he could kill me.

Since then, I have been trying to put the pieces of my life back together, which would seem like an extremely difficult task. I've got two kids to explain things to, two kids who I hope are not affected by their father's ways, through trauma that affects their lives now or is delayed and ends up seeping into their adulthood, affecting their relationships as they get older. I've also had to deal with the police and the media, all people who had so many questions and required so many answers, gruelling affairs that sapped the energy out of me, as if my traumatic time in the forest with Lachlan hadn't done that enough.

I explained I acted in self-defence when I struck him with the rock that sent him under the water, after he had pursued me through the woods with murderous intent, and based on Francesca's testimony of how dangerous Lachlan was, my version of events was trusted. It helped that I was covered in cuts and bruises from my exchange with my husband; the fall down the embankment and the ensuing scramble for survival leaving me with marks on my body that attested to my desperate fight for life. It was a relief that everyone believed me because I don't know what I would have done if they hadn't.

Then, last but not least, although it's felt like a few times recently, I've had to try and focus on myself, processing my emotions, dealing with the fact that I could have died, my children could have died, and even though I outlasted the danger in our family, that doesn't mean I've come out of it unscathed.

To this day, I feel what is known as survivor's guilt. I realise that Paisley and Teri died, and Francesca almost died, because they were not interested in Lachlan. That hurt his ego, which in turn, fuelled his desire to see them all punished. While I guess I was never really in true danger until the very end when Lachlan's past was exposed and I was trying to leave him, I have spent many nights lying awake in my bed since this all happened asking myself one very specific question.

What if I had rejected Lachlan back when we first met?

Based on what I know about him now, it's unlikely he would have taken it well. Would he have become obsessed with me like he did the others and, eventually, tried to hurt me too? I don't know because, unlike those other poor women, I welcomed his advances, which meant I was never exposed to the darker side of Lachlan Ferguson. It's frightening to think that me saying no to him could have been one of the last things I ever did. But I said yes, which led to marriage, and children, and this home we all shared together, and for many, many years, I was blissfully unaware of the danger I have so narrowly avoided. But everything comes out in the end and now I know the man he was, I can appreciate how close to death I have been for all these years.

That's exactly why, even though Lachlan is dead, making me a widow and Bonnie and William fatherless, I don't feel a void in our lives. It's easier to get past the grieving process and focus on the future when you realise you are far better off without the person who has gone. There's no doubt that my two beautiful children and I are safer now, without the monster lurking in our home, infecting our lives, acting out and hurting others while pretending to us like he was a good man.

It's been incredibly difficult facing my friends since all this happened, in particular, having them know that my husband is the reason our friendship group lost a member and I lost a dear friend. But as mortified as they were to learn that Lachlan was Teri's killer, they all see that it was not my fault, and I am as much a victim as anyone. As for Francesca, while I have never met her or spoken to her, I have read an interview she did in the news, a feature about her brush with 'The Serial Killer Next Door', and while she most likely did it for money, she spoke warmly of me, not passing on any blame, just like no blame could be attached to anyone Lachlan encountered during his reign of terror.

And what about Paisley? The Scottish teenager whose death started this whole thing, leading to a world-watched documentary and, ultimately, was the thing that prompted me to take my family to Carnfield, sparking the decline of my once-controlling husband? Her family finally have the closure they have been seeking for so long. As does Angus, the man who has had his life ruined by the constant accusations and suspicions. As for the rest of the village, they might finally be able to move on and make their home known for something else one day – something better – and I really hope that can be the case.

As I walk around my house, the one that is now devoid of any photos featuring the man I was married to, I am in search of my children. The loss of my husband has had the sting taken out of it by the fact that I now know him to be a terrible man. But there is nothing that is going to reduce the sting of seeing my daughter leave for university soon, which is why I want to spend as much time with her as possible before she goes.

I find her and her brother reclining on the sofas in front of the television, a familiar position for them both to be in, and one they have had to adopt more so than usual in recent weeks due to all the journalists camping outside our house. I've spent most of that time with them, the three of us shielding from the noise of the outside world by losing ourselves in some mindless TV shows that might be able to make us laugh and forget our troubles for a few seconds at least. But when I see what they are watching today, I realise it is not just another mindless show. That's because I recognise the person on the screen. It's Angus, speaking to the camera in his distinctive Scottish drawl.

'What's this?' I ask Bonnie and William tentatively.

'A new documentary,' William replies.

'Sorry, we just wanted to see what they were saying about us,' Bonnie adds, aware that I might not approve of this. But it's okay, we should find out what people are saying, so I take a seat on the edge of the sofa and start watching with them.

'I'm just glad justice was done,' Angus says on screen, and I note that he looks well and doesn't seem to be slurring his words, which suggests that he has got himself sober recently. I wonder if the recent redemption he has had has allowed him the peace of mind to change his ways. It must be a huge relief for him to no longer be living under a cloud of distrust. 'I regret not making my suspicions heard,' he goes on. 'I always had a feeling Lachlan had something to do with it. But I pitied myself *and my life more than trying to seek the truth for others, and that is my fault. Maybe I could have brought him to justice sooner. Then again, he was a master manipulator, so maybe not.'*

The scene changes then, switching from the shot of Angus in a quiet room to a sweeping aerial view of Carnfield. Then we're back inside another room, this one with Paisley's parents in it.

When I see Mr and Mrs Hamilton, I notice there is more of a light to their eyes, as if they have been recharged slightly after spending so many years running on low battery. That must be what getting answers does to a person, because while their daughter is still gone, they now have an understanding of why she was taken.

'We would like to thank Jenny Ferguson for the bravery she showed in protecting herself and her children from him,' Mr Hamilton says. *'If she hadn't fought him so valiantly, she may not be here now, and we may never have heard why Lachlan did what he did. But we have the truth, and we will carry that with us for the rest of our lives, until the time comes for us to join our daughter in heaven.'*

I watch as Mrs Hamilton sheds a tear then before the couple grip each other's hands, and I'm struck by the reminder that while they have lost a child and I have not, I have lost what they currently have.

Each other.

The support of a spouse.

The marital bond.

That's all gone for me. I'm widowed now, and even if Lachlan was still here, we'd be divorced. I'm all by myself. No partner to hold hands with. No ring on my finger. Nothing. But that's okay because if the price of stopping a bad man is I have to spend more time on my own, so be it. I could easily cry each morning after waking and each night before sleep, but I do my best not to because I'm determined to be strong. I don't want to spend the rest of my life as the victim. I don't deserve to live under that cloud and my departed husband certainly doesn't deserve to have that over me.

As the documentary wraps up, I see more picturesque views of the village while a narrator talks over the footage. I zone out from what they are saying because I've heard about and seen enough of that place to last me a lifetime. I'm sure the documentary makers are going to wrap all of this up with a neat little bow and that will be the end of that. But real life is never that neat and tidy and, sometimes, things can't always be wrapped up totally. A perfect example of that is the fact that while myself and the rest of the world are sure that Lachlan is dead, his body was never actually recovered from that loch.

I told the police he went below the surface, and they subsequently sent divers down to look for his body, but it was never found. A local expert then mentioned about the river that came off the loch and ran out to sea, and raised the theory that his body could have been swept out in an underwater current. If so, it might never be found. I'm struck by the similarities between my husband's life and death. I didn't know him when he existed and even now he's gone, I still feel like he is a mystery.

I try not to care because he was already dead to me the second I found out who he really was. But it would offer real finality if I had seen his corpse.

As it is, I just have to imagine it lying at the bottom of the sea somewhere, carried away by the current through the loch, down the river and out into the vast, frigid ocean that surrounds Scotland.

That's where it is.

Isn't it?

I could go on thinking that forever.

Until a knock on the door a month later changes everything...

EPILOGUE

JENNY

I stare at the man on my doorstep and almost want to rub my eyes to test if they are deceiving me.

But they are not.

He really is standing in front of me.

'Angus,' I say nervously. 'What are you doing here?'

'Can I come in?' he asks in his strong Scottish accent, and considering how far he must have travelled to get here, it would be harsh to say no. But I don't know Angus that well and the last time I saw him, he was a drunk with a grudge, so is it sensible to allow him into my home? But he appears different here, softer, more vulnerable, and for a brief second, it's like looking in a mirror and seeing a person who feels exactly like I do at this time. I could let him in but keep the door unlocked in case I need to open it again quickly. I also have my mobile in my pocket if I need to call anyone. But hopefully I won't need to do anything because Angus won't force me to. I'm also wary of somebody else on this street spotting him and recognising him from the documentary, be it a neighbour or a loitering journalist, because I don't need people gossiping any more than they already are.

'Okay,' I say, allowing him inside before the obvious question comes to my mind.

'How did you find me?'

'Your address was leaked on an online forum where people were talking about Lachlan,' Angus explains as he steps past me and into my home, and I notice that I don't detect the same hint of alcohol on his breath as I did back in Carnfield. He looks sober too, fresh and clean-cut, like he's really made an effort to turn himself around. I'm glad about that, but still wary of why he is here to see me.

'I didn't know my address was online,' I say as I close the door while considering getting the locks changed in case some crazy person on the internet with an obsession with my husband's crimes decides to start stalking me. But given how much thought I've already been putting into moving house and having a fresh start away from the memories of this place, I guess this might be the final motivation to make that move.

'Are your children home?' Angus asks, looking up the stairs, but I shake my head.

'No, it's just me,' I reply, wondering why he needed to know that, and I remain on guard as I try to figure out what this man wants.

'Good. We can talk then. But first, can I have a drink? I'm parched.'

I initially fear he is back to seeking alcohol, but he reads my mind and smiles faintly.

'A water will do fine,' he says, and I nod before heading into the kitchen.

He follows me in and waits patiently as I fill up a glass from the tap before I hand it to him and he takes a long gulp. I consider asking him how he made the journey here from Scotland, whether it was by car or by train. But it's not really important, so there's no need for small talk. There certainly isn't when Angus speaks again.

'I have to tell you something,' he says as he sets his half-empty glass down on the kitchen table. 'I considered not doing so, but it doesn't feel right to keep it from you, even if I'm taking a risk by mentioning it.'

'What is it?' I ask, my body starting to grow more tense by the second.

'It's about Lachlan.'

'What about him?'

I am dreading what Angus might say next. Is there another horror story to come out about my husband? Is there something else he did that would shock and disgust me, something from his childhood that only Angus knows about?

'I was there that day when you fought with him by the loch,' Angus admits then. 'I saw everything.'

'What?' I cry, confused as to how that could be so because we were in the middle of nowhere and there was no one else around. Or so I thought.

'I'd seen you and your family leaving Carnfield in your car,' Angus explains as he glances at a photo of Bonnie and William on one of my fridge magnets. 'I noticed how fast and erratically Lachlan was driving so I took a car from outside the mechanic's garage and followed you.'

'You stole a car?'

'Don't worry, it's not as dramatic as it sounds. The mechanic is one of the few people in the village who doesn't hate me, so he sometimes lets me take out the cars he has fixed, just to check they are working properly.'

'But you followed us? Why?'

'I was worried about you and the kids.'

I'm both surprised and touched by that statement and, as such, I don't speak, allowing Angus to go on.

'I was a little way back on the road when I saw your car stop. I parked out of sight and watched you and your children get out and enter the woods, and then I saw Lachlan leave the car and follow you in. That's when I left my own car and entered the woods too.'

Angus is talking with such conviction that I don't have any reason to doubt what he is telling me.

'I was just watching to make sure you were safe,' he tells me. 'But when I saw you were running from Lachlan, I realised the immediate danger you felt you were in, so I kept following you until I saw Lachlan catch up to you on the edge of that embankment.'

Angus now looks sorry, as if he feels he could have done more at that moment.

'I almost intervened but just before I did, you pulled Lachlan over the edge with you,' he says. 'I lost sight of you and, for a minute, I didn't know if you were alive or dead. But when I looked over the edge, I saw you both below. I saw what happened when Lachlan regained consciousness, and I saw him go under the water.'

As I listen to him recounting what I experienced, I still don't know why he feels the need to tell me this. Couldn't he have kept this to himself?

'I had to hit him. It was in self-defence,' I say, just in case Angus is going to question my use of the rock on my husband's skull.

'I know that, and you know that,' Angus replies, calming my nerves a little. 'But what you don't know is what happened after you left.'

I frown. That is a strange thing to say.

'What do you mean what happened next?' I ask urgently. 'I left to go and find my children and Lachlan was at the bottom of that loch.'

I stare at Angus as I wait for him to confirm that, but he doesn't speak.

'Right?' I say then, starting to doubt everything.

'No,' Angus says eventually with a slow shake of the head.

'You left to find your kids, but the second part is wrong. Lachlan was not at the bottom of that loch. I watched him get out of the water.'

My breath catches in my throat, and I need to grip the kitchen countertop to stop myself from potentially falling over.

'What?' I cry, fear swarming through every cell in my body.

'Lachlan was still alive when you left,' Angus grimly confirms. 'He made it back out of the loch and, by the looks of it, he was going to come after you.'

The thought of my husband doing just that, coming after me, even now, after I thought he was gone, is terrifying, and I quickly look out of the kitchen window as if I expect to see my husband standing in the back garden with a menacing look on his face.

But he's not out there.

Not yet, anyway.

'Why didn't you tell the police?' I cry then, my fear momentarily being replaced by anger at Angus. 'They could be looking for him. They could have caught him. But he could be anywhere now. He could come back and hurt me or the children!'

I suddenly feel the urge to call Bonnie and William and tell them to come home. Or maybe I should call the police first and get them to locate them because they're going to need protecting as soon as possible.

'He's not going to come back,' Angus says then, his calm voice offsetting my panic. 'He's not going to come back because I killed him.'

I stare at Angus in disbelief as he nods.

'I waited for Lachlan to make it back up the embankment and go deeper into the woods before I ambushed him. I struck him over the head with a broken branch and then I hit him several more times to make sure he really was done. After checking for a pulse and finding none, I dragged his body away, covered it in leaves and other foliage, and then left.'

I cannot believe what Angus is telling me, but he is still showing no signs of lying or embellishing.

'I stayed away until the police had conducted their search of the loch,' Angus goes on. 'I did initially wonder if the sniffer dogs might detect the body, but the search was focused on the water, not the area where the body was hidden up above the embankment and in the woods, which was a good distance away from the loch. But of course they failed to find a body in the water because there was no body in there. Only I knew where it was, and when it was safe to do so, I returned to the scene with the tools to dig a hole for Lachlan's body. He's buried now, in those woods where he chased you and your children, and he will most likely remain there undiscovered for the rest of our lives. Unless...'

Angus's voice trails off there, and while I am still reeling from what he has told me, I find my voice to ask him to finish his sentence.

'Unless what?'

'Unless you tell the police what I just told you,' Angus says before picking up his glass of water again and taking another sip. I guess that means he is done talking and now it's on me to decide where this conversation goes next.

'Why would you confess this?' I ask him, confused. 'You could have kept this a secret. I would never have known.'

'That's true,' Angus replies. 'But you would never have known for sure that Lachlan was dead either. Not without his body being found. I didn't want you to spend the rest of your life wondering if he might still be out there. I felt you deserved to know that he was definitely gone, and as he was your husband, you deserved to know exactly how he died. Or, if you were certain he was dead and were feeling any guilt about what happened, just to know that he died by my hand, not yours.'

I stare at Angus, this man who has come all the way from Scotland to not only assure me that I am forever safe from my killer husband, but also to clear my conscience of any possible guilt I might have been harbouring about taking a life. He has done this for me and now he needs something in return. He needs to know what I intend to do with the information he has given me.

'I won't tell the police,' I say firmly. 'I won't say a word of this to anybody. And I don't need to know where Lachlan's body is, nor do I wish to see it. You've already done enough for me and my family. Too much. So thank you.'

Angus nods in appreciation at my gratitude before he finishes his drink and places the empty glass down. If he wishes there had been something stronger in that glass, he doesn't let on.

'I'll be going then,' he says after a quiet moment, and I watch as he turns to leave for the door.

'Wait,' I say, feeling like I can't let him walk out of here after all he has done for me. All he has been through in his life because of Lachlan and all that he is missing in his life now because of him.

Angus turns back and looks at me, and for a second, I don't know exactly what I'm going to say to him. But then it comes to me, and while it might not be appropriate, it feels right in the moment.

'Maybe we could get a coffee or something while you're here,' I suggest.

'A coffee?'

'Yeah. My way of saying thank you.'

'You don't need to buy me a coffee to say thank you,' he says with a warm smile, and given how smartly he is dressed and how neat his hair is, I wonder if he doesn't need anybody to buy him anything these days. He must have got himself a job, possibly outside of Carnfield, in nearby Edinburgh, perhaps. I should ask him about it. Whatever he has done, he really does seem to have turned his life around. Then again, it must be very freeing to no longer have everybody think you got away with murder twenty-five years ago.

'Maybe not. But I'd like to. So what do you say? Could you stick around for a little while longer?'

I'm surprised at how much I'm hoping Angus says yes to my suggestion, but when he nods, I feel a warmth I have not felt in a long time.

It's a warmth I used to feel when I met Lachlan. A warmth that told me I could be happy with this man. I was wrong about him. But I don't feel like I am wrong about the man I am looking at now.

'I'll get my coat and we can go find a coffee shop,' I suggest. Angus seems okay with that idea, so I get myself ready, weirdly feeling a nervous apprehension as I do, as if I'm preparing myself for a first date. But this isn't a date, right?

I mean, it would be weird if I was to date the childhood best friend of my deceased, murderous husband. Then again, given what I have been through, what both Angus and I have been through, don't we deserve to do something that makes us feel happier? If we find solace in one another's company, then is that such a bad thing? And it sure would be easier to date somebody who can relate to what I've been through rather than have to explain my whole shocking backstory to a new guy one day who would most likely run a mile before we'd even finished our first drink.

I quickly check my reflection in the hallway mirror and tuck a loose strand of my hair back behind my ear, noting as I do how I'm suddenly more self-conscious about my appearance. *This is not a date*, I have to silently tell myself again.

I put on my coat and shoes before we leave my house, and as we start walking into town, I am relieved not to see any photographers lurking on my street. I guess enough time has passed for them to become occupied with other stories, so they must be pestering some other poor soul by now. But somebody might spot us together today and, if they do, there's bound to be a call to the local newspaper about the pair of us that might eventually make it into print. But despite my initial concerns about Angus being seen with me, I suddenly no longer care. So what if someone sees and speculates? It's none of their business what we do. We're simply two people who share a common bond, that bond being that we both had our lives turned upside down at the dangerous hands of Lachlan.

He was the world's worst best friend.

He was also the world's worst husband.

We walk in silence, but it's not awkward, and the further we go, the more I entertain the idea of seeing this handsome, polite and sober Scotsman again. Who knows, maybe something could happen between me and Angus one day, after we have taken things slowly, of course.

Is it weird if I end up dating the man who murdered my husband?

No, I don't think so.

After all, it wouldn't be the first time I had shared a bed with a killer, would it?

A LETTER FROM DANIEL

Dear reader,

I want to say a huge thank you for choosing to read *The Husband*. If you did enjoy it and would like to keep up to date with all my latest Bookouture releases, please sign up at the following link. Your email address will never be shared and you can unsubscribe at any time.

www.bookouture.com/daniel-hurst

I hope you loved *The Husband*, and if you did, I would be very grateful if you could write an honest review. I'd love to hear what you think!

You can read my free short story, *The Killer Wife*, by signing up to my Bookouture mailing list.

You can also visit my website where you can download a free psychological thriller called *Just One Second* and join my personal weekly newsletter, where you can hear all about my future writing as well as my adventures with my wife, Harriet, and daughter, Penny!

Thank you,

Daniel

KEEP IN TOUCH WITH DANIEL

Get in touch with me directly at my email address
daniel@danielhurstbooks.com. I reply to every message!

www.danielhurstbooks.com

 facebook.com/danielhurstbooks
 instagram.com/danielhurstbooks

PUBLISHING TEAM

Turning a manuscript into a book requires the efforts of many people. The publishing team at Bookouture would like to acknowledge everyone who contributed to this publication.

Audio
Alba Proko
Melissa Tran
Sinead O'Connor

Commercial
Lauren Morrissette
Hannah Richmond
Imogen Allport

Cover design
Lisa Horton

Data and analysis
Mark Alder
Mohamed Bussuri

Editorial
Natasha Harding
Lizzie Brien

Made in United States
Troutdale, OR
02/04/2025

28665829R00154